Gabrielle was breathless and just a tad bit giddy as they danced.

Shane guided her easily around the dance floor to the mid-tempo jazz tune. He bent down to rest his head lightly against the side of her face, and she could feel his breath against her cheek.

A slow song came on and Shane slowed the tempo. Shane closed the gap between them until they were chest-to-chest and hip-to-hip. When he ground his hips against hers, Gabrielle thought she might faint. Her cheeks became warm, and she could feel liquid heat, unlike she'd ever felt before, pooling in the lower half of her body. There was no mistaking that Shane Adams knew *exactly* what turned her on.

And when his hands reached out to caress her face, Gabrielle couldn't help but look up into his hazel eyes. She understood what she saw there: lust, plain and simple. But she never expected him to act on it. So she was surprised when Shane leaned down to brush his lips gently across hers. It was the softest of kisses, but it sent a shiver running up her spine all the same. She didn't—couldn't—stop him when he deepened the kiss.

Books by Yahrah St. John

Kimani Romance

Never Say Never
Risky Business of Love
Playing for Keeps
This Time for Real
If You So Desire
Two to Tango
Need You Now
Lost Without You

YAHRAH ST. JOHN

is the author of ten books and numerous short stories. A graduate of Hyde Park Career Academy, she earned a bachelor of arts degree in English from Northwestern University.

Her books have garnered four-star ratings from *RT Book Reviews, Rawsistaz Reviewers, Romance in Color* and numerous book clubs. A member of Romance Writers of America, St. John is an avid reader of all genres. She enjoys the arts, cooking, traveling, basketball and adventure sports, but her true passion remains writing.

St. John lives in sunny Orlando, the City Beautiful.

Lost Without YOU

YAHRAH ST. JOHN

KIMANI
ROMANCE

Dedicated to my Dad, Austin Mitchell, for believing
I could reach my goal of seeing my 10th book in print.

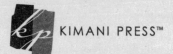 KIMANI PRESS™

ISBN-13: 978-0-373-86257-3

Recycling programs
for this product may
not exist in your area.

LOST WITHOUT YOU

Copyright © 2012 by Yahrah Yisrael

www.kimanipress.com

Printed in U.S.A.

Dear Reader,

Lost Without You continues the Adams saga introduced previously in *Need You Now,* but will focus on Shane Adams and Gabrielle Burton. When I originally conceived the book, it started out as a makeover story: Gabrielle as the prudish chemist and Shane as the gorgeous bachelor. It quickly evolved into more, with the epic rivalry between Adams Cosmetics and Jax Cosmetics as the backdrop.

Since fragrance played a big role, I realized a great conflict would be to have the fragrance stolen and have Gabrielle appear to be the culprit.

Remember the spoiler alert I gave you about Andrew Jackson of Jax Cosmetics? He is back in a major way as the villain of *Lost Without You.* So you can only imagine what will happen when his estranged son, real-estate mogul Jasper Jackson, falls in love with sexy spokesmodel, Courtney Adams. Stay tuned for the final chapter of the An Adams Affair trilogy, *Formula for Passion,* coming September 2012.

Visit my website at www.yahrahstjohn.com for the latest updates or contact me via email at Yahrah@yahrahstjohn.com.

Warm regards,

Yahrah St. John

I couldn't have reached my goal of publishing my 10th book without the love and support of all my family, friends and readers. Thank you for continuing to allow me to do what I love, and that's bringing you stories of love, passion, drama and intrigue. I hope to bring you more great books in the future as I challenge myself to reach new heights as an author.

Chapter 1

"Thanks to Hypnotic and the backing of Graham International, Adams Cosmetics is back in the black!" Kayla Graham announced during a midweek board meeting in early March at the Adams Cosmetics corporate office in Atlanta. "The holiday sales numbers are in and the outlook is promising. We are beating our competition, Jax Cosmetics, in every division from cosmetics to skin care to fragrance."

"Was there ever any doubt?" Shane asked.

Kayla smiled at her brother's confidence. "Of course not, we—" she pointed to the other family members present: her husband, Ethan Graham, and younger sister Courtney "—know how talented you are."

Shane had graduated at the top of his class at the Fashion Institute of Technology with a bachelor of science degree in cosmetics and fragrance marketing. He'd then gone to perfumery school in Paris before apprenticing at the Fragonard perfumery in Grasse, France.

Kayla knew her brother was well trained to bring Adams Cosmetics into the twenty-first century, but he needed help. He'd already been spearheading developing new products for the past six years, but they couldn't continue to rely solely on him. Otherwise, he would burn out.

"Thank you," Shane replied. "Andrew Jackson must be spinning on those alligator heels of his."

Andrew Jackson owned Jax Cosmetics, their main competitor. Theirs was a bitter rivalry that spanned back to the days when their father, Byron, and mother, Elizabeth, went to college together. Their mother used to date Andrew, and when she chose Byron over Andrew, the feud began.

"We need to capitalize on the momentum Hypnotic is bringing," Ethan Graham said as he joined the conversation. He was happy to see that Adams Cosmetics was finally starting to break even. It would make his board of directors very happy, considering they hadn't been pleased when he'd decided to purchase Adams Cosmetics last year for his company, Graham International. He hadn't cared, though, because thanks to his acquisition, he'd fallen in love with Kayla and she was expecting their first child, a son, in a few months.

"I couldn't agree more," Shane returned. "I'm working on the next fragrance."

"How's it coming along?" Courtney inquired.

Shane rubbed his goatee thoughtfully. "It's coming." Truth be told, he was having a hard time coming up with just the right notes to finish the fragrance on top of all his other work.

"We don't mean to pressure you." Kayla could see the tense look on Shane's face. "But we're hot now."

"I'm well aware of that fact."

"Is there anything we can do to help?" Courtney asked.

She wasn't good with chemistry, but she had a degree in marketing and finance.

"I have a solution," Ethan stated.

Kayla turned and looked at her husband. They'd discussed his solution at length over the past several days. She'd hoped that Shane would have better news about his progress, but since he didn't, they didn't have much choice but to proceed with Ethan's suggestion. Kayla held her breath and braced herself for the blowup she knew was about to come.

"Oh, yeah?" Shane swiveled around in his chair to face Ethan. "What's that?"

"We bring in another head chemist."

Shane jumped to his feet. "What the hell did you just say?"

Ethan held up his hand. "Shane, listen. This would help to ease the load on your shoulders." He knew this decision would be met with hostility, much as his decision last year to remove Courtney as the Adams spokesmodel had. Hiring his ex-girlfriend, Noelle Warner, as her replacement had proved disastrous and had nearly destroyed his marriage and cost him his child. This time, he'd consulted Kayla, and she'd been in agreement that giving Shane some relief was in the best interest of the company.

"I don't need to ease my load," Shane replied harshly. "I had been running the cosmetics and fragrance lab for six years before Graham International ever came along."

"Shane, this is in no way a condemnation of your work," Kayla responded. "Everyone needs help every now and then."

"I don't need any help."

"Yet, you haven't come up with a new fragrance even though you've been working on it for several months," Ethan returned.

"In case you haven't noticed, I have created several new lipsticks, shadows and nail polishes for the cosmetics division in that same time." He didn't appreciate Ethan honing in on his territory. Just because he'd learned to get along with his brother-in-law did not mean he'd forgotten how Ethan had come to own half of Adams Cosmetics.

Ethan sighed. "Of course we've noticed what a great job you've done with cosmetics, but I also think giving you some help is needed. We all want to see Adams Cosmetics thrive and expand, and that can't happen if you're being stretched too thin."

Shane turned to his sister. "Are you in agreement with this?"

Kayla hated when Shane's hazel eyes pierced hers. Sometimes it was as if he could see right through her. She reached across the table and grasped Ethan's hand in hers. Last year, they had made a pact to run the company as equals and share in the decision making. "Yes, we are."

Shane rose and shrugged his shoulders. "Fine. I've been outvoted. Why is that always the case with you, Ethan?"

Ethan was about to speak, but Kayla touched his arm.

"Shane, please don't be angry with us."

"And may I ask whom you've chosen as my counterpart?"

"Shane, we would never choose someone without your input. You're the one who has to work with them on a day-to-day basis. It's your lab."

"How gracious of you," Shane replied sarcastically.

"But we do have a candidate in mind," Ethan added.

"Enough with the suspense," Courtney said with a sigh. She'd been silent for long enough. "Just spit it out."

"Gabrielle Burton."

* * *

Shane paced the laboratory floor. Of all the names he'd expected to hear, Gabrielle Burton was not one of them. She was an excellent chemist, but she was also his archrival. They'd gone to perfumery school together and no matter the forum, the five-foot-six brunette had always competed against him.

Once near the end of the term, they'd competed to see who created the best fragrance. Their peers had to vote on their favorite scent. Shane and Gabrielle had tied for first place, but Gabrielle had insisted on a recount as she was sure she'd win, because her fragrance was better, she'd taunted. She'd been wrong. A recount had discovered one missing vote, giving Shane the win. What surprised him the most was that she'd merely shook his hand and told him she'd beat him the next time.

She'd been an annoyance, to say the least, and had rubbed Shane the wrong way from day one. If he said the sky was blue, she would say it was green, if only to be obstinate. Shane highly doubted Gabrielle Burton would accept having to answer to him in the lab. He'd heard she'd stayed in Paris to work for L'Oréal, but that wouldn't stop her from going after this position.

This was definitely going to be interesting.

"Gabby, are you sure you want to leave Paris?" Mariah asked as she watched her dear friend and roommate pack her suitcases that evening. They'd met ten years ago when Gabrielle was lost on the Paris subway. With some free time on her hands, Mariah had graciously agreed to show her the way. Born and raised in South Africa, Mariah had been a struggling model back then, but now was one of the most sought-after models. With Mariah always on the road, it hadn't made sense for her to pay for her own place, and so they'd moved in together. A decade later, they were still the best of friends.

"Yes, I think it's finally time I go back to the States," Gabrielle said, exiting her closet with several handfuls of clothes. "I can't run from my past forever."

Ten years ago, she had come to Paris for perfumery school and had never gone back to the United States. She had never faced down the fact that she'd lost her brother, Seth, in a tragic drowning accident when she was fifteen. She'd insisted on accompanying Seth on a boating trip with his friends. Then the weather turned treacherous when they were on their way back to shore, and Gabrielle had fallen overboard. Seth had jumped in to save her. And he had; he just hadn't been able to save himself.

Their family had never recovered from the loss. Although they'd never said it, Gabrielle knew her parents blamed her for losing their only son, and having her around only seemed to add to her parents' grief. So as soon as she could, Gabrielle had hightailed it out of Atlanta, come to Paris and stayed.

She'd graduated top of her class in perfumery school and had been immediately hired by L'Oréal. Although she was an excellent chemist, she'd recently been overlooked for a promotion. Gabrielle supposed she didn't have the look or pizzazz they wanted in their top-chemist position, and so she'd begun to realize it was time for a change. She hoped that a new opportunity with Adams Cosmetics would give her the creative boost she needed.

Of course, the position meant she would have to work closely with Shane Adams, and that caused Gabrielle to take a deep, calming breath. The knowledge that she would be going to work for her father's employer's direct competition was not lost on her. Not many people knew that her father, James Burton, had started out as an assistant at Jax Cosmetics. He had moved up the ranks and was now an executive. When she was younger, he used to sneak her and Seth into the labs at night, and it was there that she developed her interest in chemistry.

And the fact that she and Shane had been like oil and water in perfumery school made the position even more of a challenge. But despite their rivalry and her personal conflict, Gabrielle was sure they could overcome their differences. They were both professionals, after all.

"Okay, so you're interviewing, but why are you packing?" Mariah asked. "You haven't even been offered the position."

"That's irrelevant, because I will be."

"You're that sure of yourself?"

Gabrielle spun on her heels to face her friend. "Of course I am. My credentials are above reproach. I have a degree in chemistry and went to the top perfumery school. Shane Adams will have to acknowledge that." Ethan Graham had called and informed her that, although she was on the short list, it was ultimately Shane's decision whether he would hire her or not.

"*The* Shane Adams?" Mariah smiled knowingly. "Your rival in perfumery school?" Mariah remembered Gabrielle mentioning the sexy Atlanta bachelor.

"Yes." Gabrielle turned back around to continue packing.

"Who just so happens to be handsome as sin," Mariah replied.

"Shane?" Gabrielle's voice rose despite herself. "Handsome? I hadn't noticed." She attempted to fold her blouse into a perfect square, but found it hard to do so. She hated for things to be out of order. Some would say she had a slight case of OCD.

"Oh, really?" Mariah picked up a nearby fashion magazine and flipped through several pages. She stopped when she found a picture of Shane and his sister Kayla celebrating the launch of their new fragrance, Hypnotic. She rose from the chair and came to Gabrielle's side, placing the magazine in her line of sight. "Don't tell me you hadn't noticed how devastatingly handsome this man is. Because if you do, I'll know you're lying. I mean, what woman could resist that curly hair or those arresting hazel eyes?"

"I could and I have." Gabrielle pushed the magazine aside and stood up straight. "Shane was known to be a player in school, but I was much too interested in my studies to pay him any mind."

"So you competed with him instead to get his attention?"

Color flushed in Gabrielle's face. "No...no, that wasn't how it was."

Mariah's brow rose. "No?"

"No," Gabrielle stated more adamantly. "I refused to be one of Shane's little playthings that he could toss aside when he was done." Though Gabrielle had to admit there was some small part of her that had wondered what it would be like to be with a man that fine.

But the Shane Adamses of the world would never look at her. She didn't play up to their male fantasies and dress to show off her figure or cake her face with makeup. Gabrielle recognized it was ironic that she'd ended up in the fragrance and cosmetics industry, given her affinity for not wearing any.

"If you say so," Mariah said with a laugh. "I just can't imagine not wanting to try that man on for size."

Gabrielle took the blouse she'd been trying to fold and hit Mariah. "You're incorrigible."

"And you love me for it."

"I do." Gabrielle smiled. "And I will miss you dearly. Promise me you will come visit?"

"Cross my heart."

"Who is this Gabrielle Burton anyway?" Byron Adams asked his family at the dinner table. They were all seated in the grand dining room at the Adams family's eleven-room mansion having a three-course meal their cook had prepared.

"Don't you remember the emails, Daddy?" Courtney asked. "The ones from Shane?" She inclined her head in her brother's direction across the table. "I think the exact quote was, 'She's a prim and proper know-it-all who thinks she's better than me, but I'm ten times the chemist she could ever be.'"

"I was right," Shane replied. "I won best fragrance in our last year of school, and I am head of R&D of Adams Cosmetics. And she's second in command over at L'Oréal Paris."

"Are you saying she's not qualified, son?"

Shane reached for his wineglass and took a sip. "No, she's qualified."

"He just doesn't want anyone looking over his shoulder," Courtney responded.

"I think you and your sister could learn a lesson in sharing," Elizabeth Adams said from the opposite head of the table from her husband. "I recall Kayla had the same problem working with Ethan."

Byron huffed from his side of the table. "That wasn't the same thing." Although he and his son-in-law had come to a truce over the past few months, Byron had not forgotten how Ethan became a member of the family. His hostile takeover of Adams Cosmetics had nearly caused a rift in their tight-knit family. It was only when Byron realized Ethan truly loved his daughter Kayla that peace had come. It hadn't hurt either that Ethan had given Kayla back enough shares to make them equal partners in Adams Cosmetics.

"You're right, it wasn't the same thing, but the outcome can be. Ethan and Kayla are working great together at the helm of A.C. And you, Shane, could learn a lesson in humility. You can't do it all," Elizabeth said.

"I know that, Mom." Shane sighed wearily. For some reason, she could always get through to him. "I recognize that I've been working a lot of overtime, but you know as well as I do that's who I am. I'm driven to make sure we get Adams Cosmetics out of the slump."

"And you will," Elizabeth stated emphatically, reaching over the table and squeezing her son's hand. "We're just giving you some help."

"I just wish it wasn't Gabrielle Burton."

"Perhaps she's changed," Courtney offered.

Shane thought back to the bossy diva with the pencil in her perfectly coiffed updo, two-piece cardigan set and trousers leaning over his chemistry table. He doubted she'd changed at all.

Butterflies were jumping up and down in Gabrielle's stomach as she waited in the hall to meet with Ethan Graham, his wife, Kayla, and Shane Adams on Friday morning. Although Ethan had pretty much guaranteed her the job, she was nervous about Shane having the final sign-off.

It didn't help that she was operating on very little sleep. She'd flown in the day before and arrived in the evening. Once she'd made it to her hotel room, she was wide awake because she was still on Paris time. Gabrielle could only hope that the smug, self-entitled playboy she once knew had mellowed as the years had gone by.

Shane sat at the head of the conference-room table, waiting for Gabrielle Burton's arrival. His head was bent as he gave her resume one more cursory review, when a pair of shapely caramel legs came into his view.

Slowly, his eyes made their way from the legs to the sensible gray knee-length skirt and matching long-sleeve jacket with a lavender scarf tied around her neck. What she was wearing was perfectly suitable for an interview, but heaven forbid the woman actually show a few curves. He liked a woman who wasn't afraid to show off her God-given assets, and that definitely wasn't Gabrielle Burton.

But she had a natural beauty, which he supposed was why her nut-brown complexion was clear and her face was free of makeup. She wore her hair in a simple French twist. Oh, yes, this was exactly the woman he remembered.

Ethan and Shane both rose from their seats, but Ethan was the first to speak. "Gabrielle, glad you could make it here for an in-person interview. I hope your flight was pleasant."

"Pleasant?" Gabrielle chuckled. "It was more than pleasant." She'd never been in anything so divine. "You really didn't have to send your private jet."

"It was my pleasure," Ethan stated. He turned to his side. "This is my wife, Kayla Graham."

"Pleasure to meet you." Gabrielle shook her hand. Kayla Adams was several inches taller than her, with flaw-less mocha skin, curly hair that nearly reached her shoul-ders and a clearly pregnant belly.

Gabrielle turned and braced herself for seeing Shane Adams again after nearly a decade. He was every bit as fine as he'd been back then, maybe more so. He towered over her at six feet with a short curly afro, creamy café-au-lait skin, hazel eyes and full, sexy lips. She could tell that a sculpted body lay underneath his Italian suit.

"Gabby." Shane nodded at her. "You're looking well."

Gabrielle hadn't expected such a friendly greeting, given they'd been rivals in school. "No one's called me that for a long time."

"I hope you don't mind me using your nickname. Gabrielle just seems so formal." Shane smirked, knowing she hated it. In school, she'd said the nickname Gabby reminded her of some airhead name like Buffy, and she'd refused to answer to it.

Gabrielle swallowed hard at having those sensuous eyes staring at her so intently. "Well, I do prefer Gabrielle."

"As you wish." Shane watched her sit down and cross her legs all the while pulling down her skirt. It made Shane wonder what it was she was hiding underneath.

"Well, we are happy to have someone of your caliber interested in Adams Cosmetics," Kayla said, trying to ease the obvious tension between the two chemists. Courtney had reminded her that Shane and Gabrielle were not fans of each other.

"Your resume is quite impressive," Ethan stated.

"Thank you," Gabrielle said and smiled. "I believe in working hard to achieve one's goals."

"After you graduated *second* in your class at perfumery school, you joined L'Oréal?" Shane jumped right into the fray.

Gabrielle stared daggers at Shane. Trust him to remind her that he'd beaten her as valedictorian of their class. Had he called her Gabby to knock her off her game? "That's correct. And I've enjoyed an immensely successful career there."

"Why don't you tell me some of the projects you've

worked on?" Shane asked. It was time to skip the pleasantries and get down to business. Find out exactly what Gabrielle Burton was made of.

"Well, I've worked on numerous L'Oréal fragrances, and recently we've been working on some new skin-firming crèmes."

"Tell me more," Shane urged.

For the next hour, Shane grilled Gabrielle about her work in the lab. When he was done, he was impressed with her credentials, but he wasn't about to tell her that, at least not yet. Gabrielle was competitive and would be eager to prove her worth.

Kayla watched Shane and couldn't believe how hard her brother was being on Gabrielle. She had never seen him behave this way toward a woman. Usually Shane was such a smooth talker that women melted around him like butter. Gabrielle seemed immune to Shane.

"One final question," Shane said. "Do you really feel confident working in cosmetics even though your primary focus was fragrance?"

"I am a qualified chemist," Gabrielle stated. She resented that Shane was implying otherwise. "And I am confident that I can work on cosmetics or fragrances."

"That's good to know." Shane's gaze focused on Gabrielle. "Because this company means everything to me, and I will not settle for mediocrity."

"Wow!" Ethan looked down at his watch. "Look at the time. I have to get to another meeting. Ms. Burton, we're delighted to have met you and will be making our final decision within the next few days. We'll be in touch."

"Thank you, Mr. Graham." Gabrielle rose from the table and shook his hand. "Mrs. Graham." She snapped up her portfolio before turning to Shane. "Mr. Adams." She called him by his formal name. "It was a pleasure to get reacquainted with you, and I do so hope for the opportunity to work with you."

Shane smiled and nodded. *He just bet she did.*

Once Gabrielle had gone, Kayla turned to Shane. "Was that really necessary?"

"What?" Shane asked.

"You cross-examined her as if she was on the witness stand," Kayla responded. "You know as well as I do that Gabrielle Burton is more than qualified for this job."

"I had to be sure she wanted the position," Shane replied. "And if she was willing to fight for it."

"And I assume you got your answer?" Ethan asked.

"She will do." Shane closed the folder holding her resume.

"Then why don't you tell her she got the position?"

"We are not interviewing anyone else?" Shane asked, slapping down the folder on the table. "I should have known this was a done deal with you and Ethan, because you always have to have your way."

"That's not true." Kayla leaped to defend her husband.

"Shane, you know this was merely a formality to get your stamp of approval, which she has. You yourself said she's qualified for the position. So go give her the good news, as she will be your employee." Ethan rose from his chair because the discussion was over. "Kayla and I have other plans. My dear…" He turned to help his pregnant wife out of the seat. "Let us know a start date," Ethan said over his shoulder on their way out.

Shane wrung his hands as he rode the hotel elevator up to Gabrielle Burton's room. He could wring his brother-in-law's neck for forcing him to have Gabrielle in his crosshairs every day. Gabrielle was competent and focused, but she was also very much by the numbers, and sometimes when it came to creating fragrances, an element of whimsy was required. He doubted Gabrielle had ever had a whimsical moment in her entire structured life.

He could have delivered the news over the telephone, but Shane preferred to take his hits like a man. Even more than that, he needed to make a few things clear to Gabrielle before she accepted the position. He didn't want there to be any misunderstandings in the future.

He arrived at her hotel room shortly after 6:00 p.m., after he'd learned from Kayla's assistant, Myra, where Gabrielle was staying. He knocked several times and was just about to leave when Gabrielle finally opened the door.

He must have awakened her, because for the first time he could remember, Gabrielle looked disheveled. Her normally perfect updo hung haphazardly over her shoulders, and the silk blouse she must have worn earlier underneath the hideous gray jacket was wrinkled. But her liquid brown eyes shone brightly, and that appealed to him.

"Shane!" Gabrielle immediately closed the door and leaned back to check herself in the foyer mirror.

"Ohmigod, I look a fright," Gabrielle said aloud. "Uh… I'll be right with you," she yelled through the door and rushed to the bathroom to find her brush and repair the damage from her afternoon nap. She was still getting accustomed to the time change and must have fallen asleep.

On the other side of the door, Shane chuckled. Gabrielle Burton not perfectly in control at all times? Heaven forbid!

When she was satisfied with the results of her impromptu hair fix and quick lip-gloss application, Gabrielle opened the door. She found Shane leaning against a pillar, looking as cool and handsome as he pleased. His hazel eyes were lit from within with a golden glow.

"Sorry for the delay. Please do come in," Gabrielle said formally.

"If now isn't a good time I can always come back," Shane said, smiling as he stood up straight.

"No…no, now is fine." Gabrielle motioned for him to come inside. "My apologies… I took a nap. I'm still trying to get on East Coast time."

Once inside the hotel room, Shane's male energy dominated the small living area, and she found it disconcerting. She watched him assess the suite before turning his eyes back on her.

He had a way of sizing her up that Gabrielle wasn't quite sure what to make of. "So, to what do I owe the honor of your visit?" Gabrielle folded her arms across her chest as a defense. "I'm sure it's not to catch up on old times."

Shane's eyes pierced hers. "And if it were?"

"Well, we were never really friends in perfumery school, now were we?" she muttered hastily.

"So we were enemies?"

Color flushed Gabrielle's cheeks. "I…I wouldn't say enemies, that's quite indelicate. I would say more like rivals."

"Hmm…" Shane mulled her comment over in his head. "And do you think you can work *under* me, your former rival?" He doubted she wanted to be *under* him for any reason.

"If that's what the job entails, but I had more hoped it would be a collaborative effort, given my background and experience."

At this, Shane's face turned as hard as stone. "Make no mistake, *I* run the lab."

Gabrielle sucked in a deep breath, as she'd obviously hit a nerve. She didn't want ego to get in the way of her getting this position, so she said, "I'm sorry. I didn't mean to infer otherwise. I just assumed we would work very closely on projects together, but ultimately you would have the final say."

"That's correct," Shane said coldly. "An *Adams* will always run Adams Cosmetics. If you are clear with those terms, then the job is yours."

A smile spread across Gabrielle's face. The news was music to her ears. She was ready to come home. "Thank you so much." She offered her hand to Shane. He stared at her small, delicate hand for several moments, as if he wasn't quite sure what he'd signed up for, before he finally shook it.

A strange electric sensation pulsed ever so briefly between them at the touch of their palms, but then it was over just as quickly as it had begun, making Gabrielle think she'd imagined the connection.

"Welcome aboard, Gabby Burton," Shane returned. He offered her a forgiving smile with no trace of his former animosity.

"Will I see you bright and early on Monday at the lab?"

"Absolutely."

Chapter 2

Gabrielle dressed with care on Monday morning as she prepared for her first day at Adams Cosmetics. She pulled her hair into an unsophisticated ponytail and donned a charcoal designer pantsuit. Because the science lab was a male-dominated place, Gabrielle wanted Shane to view her as a serious chemist. If she showed more skin or dressed to gain their attention, they might view her as inferior. But Gabrielle was determined to command Shane's respect.

She had a few last-minute jitters, but it wasn't because of her laboratory experience. She was more comfortable there than anyplace else. She was just anxious because Shane Adams had already made it clear that the lab was his domain and that he was merely tolerating her presence, much like a child who should be seen and not heard.

It didn't help that he was sinfully gorgeous. She'd acted as if she hadn't noticed with Mariah, but the truth of the matter was that she'd always known Shane Adams was attractive. It was hard not to notice him. He oozed masculinity from his every pore. Add the sexy eyes and a body for lovemaking, and any woman would be powerless to resist his charm. Except her.

Why? Because even though he was attractive, he was still the arrogant, cocky ladies' man she remembered from school. Back then, Shane had to have a woman on his arm, and even though he didn't go through women once a week as some playboys would, after several months he always seemed to tire of them, and it was on to the next.

What surprised Gabrielle the most was that after it was over, the women never spoke ill of Shane. They always praised him for respecting them and treating them well. They even said he was the most romantic man they'd ever met. How could they be so naive? Why would they date a man knowing he offered them nothing but a temporary good time? Once he'd gotten what he wanted and had his fill, the door revolved and another woman was in play.

It boggled Gabrielle's mind, and so as she walked into the laboratory that morning, she resolved that despite Shane's good looks and obvious charm, she would not be taken in by him.

Gabrielle tore through the double doors of the laboratory with gusto and stopped dead in her tracks when she saw Shane leaning over the counter smelling several vials. From her vantage point, she could see he had a well-defined behind. *Resisting his charm was going to be easier said than done.*

"So glad you could make it, Ms. Burton," Shane said, standing upright.

Gabrielle glanced down at her watch. Was she late? He did say 8:00 a.m.? "Did I miss something?" But when she looked around, she saw that several employees were already milling about in lab coats.

"No," Shane replied, walking over to the other vials he'd been working on. "But if you want to hang with this crew, you're going to have to get here earlier, my dear."

Gabrielle rolled her eyes upward. She hated the condescending tone in Shane's voice, but it was her first day and she didn't want to get on his bad side. "I will be sure to remember that." She walked closer to him until they were nearly inches apart. Being this close to Shane allowed her to smell his aftershave, which was sharp and kind of spicy. It tantalized her senses and sent shivers up and down her spine. "What are you working on?"

Shane's body instantly became alert at Gabrielle's nearness, and he stiffened. "I'm working on a couple of different scents that might work for the new fragrance."

"Really." Gabrielle walked around the counter and went to several vials containing essential oils and perfumer's alcohol. "Hmm...not bad," she said.

"I don't recall asking for your opinion," Shane replied to her lackluster response.

"And I wasn't giving you one," Gabrielle responded in turn. "I was merely commenting aloud." She grasped a sheet of perfume paper and dipped it into one of the vials. She brought the paper to her nose and inhaled deeply. After several moments she smelled it again and was silent before saying, "Seems like you're going for more of a citrus scent. Have you considered adding some spearmint?"

Shane's forehead bunched into a frown. "No, I hadn't thought of that." And he hated that she had a point, as it would complement the current potion in the vial.

"And what are these?" Gabrielle motioned to several mockups for the skin-care line.

"Some preliminaries for a redesign of the current bottle

to go along with a couple of new fragrances for the shower gels and lotions we're developing."

"So let me get this straight. You work on cosmetics, skin care and fragrances, and you only have four other employees?" Gabrielle asked.

Shane glared at her. "That's right."

"Well, no wonder you need me." Gabrielle didn't turn away from his stare. Instead, she gave him one of her own.

"*I* don't need you," Shane replied. "This lab has been working perfectly fine without you."

"Mr. Graham didn't think so."

"Because Mr. Graham isn't familiar with how the Adamses do business. We are a small family company."

"That's now a subsidiary of a major conglomerate like Graham International," Gabrielle said. "You're going to have to let go of the reins, Shane, if you want Adams Cosmetics to expand."

"How insightful of you, Gabby," Shane said, calling her by the nickname she hated. "Why don't you go check in with HR on the third floor and complete your paperwork and be back here in, say, an hour?"

"All right." Gabrielle gave Shane a halfhearted smile even though she'd rather strangle him. He was really only dismissing her because he hadn't liked what she had to say. "I'll see you shortly."

The paperwork wouldn't take Gabrielle long, but it would give Shane time to regain his composure. He wasn't used to having someone question what he was doing or what he was working on, and he didn't like it one bit. When he'd come up with a revolutionary skin-care cream seven years ago, Kayla had pretty much handed him the reins of the laboratory, and he'd never looked back. Some may have thought his sister crazy for handing over the laboratory to a twenty-five-year-old straight out of his apprenticeship, but Shane had had a vision even then, and he'd let no one deter him. So he certainly didn't appreciate Ethan bringing an outsider into his domain.

He didn't know what it was about Gabrielle that irked him so. Was it her perfectly coiffed hair? Or was it her smooth complexion free of makeup that bothered him? Or the fact that she dressed in black, browns and grays? Did the woman even own an item of color? Or perhaps it was the fact that she was the only woman on the planet who seemed immune to him.

In school, Gabrielle Burton had steered clear of him, which had only intrigued him more and made him curious to get under that layer of cool reserve. He'd watched her date Preston, a pretentious yuppie with a moneyed background who was clearly a boring dud. Yet, she'd acted as if he was the catch of the century, when in fact the relationship hadn't lasted much longer than a few months. Perhaps she liked stuck-up men who wouldn't know fun if it was staring them in the face.

Either way, Shane was not too happy about her presence, which is why he left his lab to go to Kayla's office. He had a bone to pick with his traitorous sister.

"Hi, Myra." He smiled at Kayla's assistant before heading straight into his sister's office.

Kayla was on the phone, but she waved him inside. Shane plopped down in the plush chair in front of her desk and glared at her.

Several minutes later, Kayla hung up the line. "So did you come in here to give me hell?"

"As you knew I would," Shane returned. "How could you not have given me a heads-up on what you and Ethan were discussing? I'm your brother, for Christ's sake!"

"Shane…" Kayla sighed. She knew her brother would

be upset, but she'd hoped that once he'd had time to cool down he'd see the rationale behind their decision.

"Don't 'Shane' me," he responded, jumping to his feet. "You knew I wouldn't be behind this—" he pointed to his sister "—so you and your hubby blindsided me. And I don't appreciate it."

Kayla took offense to Shane's tone. She knew the family still didn't completely trust Ethan, but she wouldn't abide Shane bad-mouthing the father of her child. "*We* did what was best for this company, and you might do well to remember that."

Shane's eyes narrowed. "Are you pulling rank on me?" Although Kayla was president of Adams Cosmetics, he was vice president and they'd always shared the same vision of what was right, until now.

"Of course not." Kayla sighed wearily and rubbed her belly. "But even you must see the logic."

"I see my territory being intruded upon by an outsider."

"Ah, now we get down to the heart of the matter," Kayla said. "It's not that we brought on some help. It's *who* we hired."

"I don't know what you're talking about."

Kayla smiled at her brother's outright lie. He wouldn't be in her office right now if Gabrielle Burton hadn't rubbed him the wrong way. "What did she do?"

"She had the nerve to tell me what note to add into my fragrance. Can you believe that?" Shane asked.

Kayla chuckled. "She is there to help you."

"I don't need her help. I have been making fragrances long before she got here."

"But haven't you said something is missing?"

Shane narrowed his eyes. "Don't use my words against me, Kay."

Kayla rose from her chair and walked over to her

brother and gave him a punch in the shoulder. "Then don't be a Neanderthal. Let the woman help you. That's what we hired her to do."

Gabrielle was on her way back from HR, with her head still focused on the mountain of paperwork she had to complete, when she bumped into someone coming out of the elevator. The papers in her hand went flying through the air and onto the floor.

"I'm so sorry," Gabrielle gushed as she bent down to pick up the papers. She glanced up to find a statuesque beauty staring down at her in what was no doubt a white designer pantsuit. Gabrielle had seen some gorgeous models in Paris, but this woman was different. She was nearly six feet tall with a short, sleek bob and arresting green eyes. Even though her makeup was immaculate, she didn't need it. She was stunning already.

"No worries, I was texting," Courtney said. "And you know what they say, you shouldn't walk and text." She bent down to help Gabrielle gather the papers strewn across the floor.

Courtney rose and handed the pile to the woman, who appeared a little bit frazzled. And what the heck was with the ponytail and drab pantsuit she was wearing? Didn't she realize what industry they were in? "By the way, my name is Courtney. Courtney Adams."

"Adams," Gabrielle said, staring back at her. "You wouldn't be any relation to Shane Adams, would you?"

Courtney smiled broadly. "Yes, he's my brother."

Gabrielle's mouth formed an O. She extended her hand. "Great to meet you. My name is Gabrielle Burton."

Courtney's eyes widened. "Ah, so you're Gabrielle Burton." She accepted the handshake.

"I see my reputation has preceded me."

"Something like that," Courtney said and laughed. "Where you off to?"

"Back to the lab," Gabrielle said, pressing the elevator call button, "where I'm sure your brother is waiting for me and ready to give me the riot act. HR took a little longer than expected."

"Is Shane giving you a hard time?"

Gabrielle gulped. She hadn't meant to speak so openly. Although she wasn't working directly with Courtney, she had done her research and knew she sat on the board of directors and was spokeswoman for the company. "No… uh…I'm sorry, I didn't mean it like that."

"Don't backpedal now," Courtney responded. "I respect a woman who can speak her mind, and I know Shane wasn't too happy to add you to his staff."

The elevator arrived at that exact moment, and Courtney joined Gabrielle on the way down to the lab.

"Good. Because I know Mr. Adams isn't happy to have me here, but I promise I will do the job to the best of my ability."

"I'm sure you will," Courtney replied. "But might I give you a word of advice?"

"Hmm…what's that?" Gabrielle glanced up at Courtney, wide-eyed.

"The first step would be to change your appearance."

"Excuse me?" Gabrielle was taken aback. "What's wrong with what I have on?"

Courtney's brow rose. "Do you *really* want me to go there?"

Gabrielle couldn't help but laugh, which immediately eased the tension she was feeling over Courtney's over-zealous tongue.

The elevator announced Gabrielle's floor and she moved toward the exit, but Courtney touched her arm.

"Listen, I have to get to a meeting," Courtney said, "but why don't we talk more over lunch?"

"Really?"

"Sure. I'll meet you in the lobby at 1:00 p.m. We'll go someplace special."

And with that comment, the elevator doors closed, leaving Gabrielle to marvel at how nice Shane's sister was compared with him.

Shane wasn't in the lab when Gabrielle arrived, so she had a few minutes to check her cell phone. She was surprised to see she'd missed a call. The voice mail was from her father, who indicated he'd heard she was back in town and wondered if she intended to come and say hello. The tone was accusatory, as if she wouldn't have come by to visit. And how the heck had he "heard" she was back in town?

She didn't have time to ponder the thought because Shane came sauntering into the lab. He strode purposely toward her, and Gabrielle couldn't help but be mesmerized at just how attractive her boss truly was. Shane had a way about him that commanded attention.

"Listen, we probably got off on the wrong foot this morning," Shane began once he reached her desk. When Gabrielle didn't stop him, he continued. "So how about we call a truce and get along? There is a lot of work to be done. You ready to roll up your sleeves?"

"Lead the way," Gabrielle said.

Over the next couple of hours, Shane introduced her to the other staff members whom she would oversee, but made it clear that the buck stopped with him. She was second in command.

Lunch came surprisingly fast and Gabrielle had to

admit she was looking forward to eating with Courtney. Despite the fact that, prior to its acquisition by Graham International, Adams Cosmetics had been considered a boutique cosmetics firm, there had been plenty of write-ups about Courtney as a spokesmodel. Courtney attended the latest industry events and fashion shows and kept Adams Cosmetics in the public eye. It had caused quite a stir in the community when the company hired the actress Noelle Warner as the face of its first fragrance, Hypnotic.

All five foot ten of Courtney was waiting for her in the lobby. She looked poised and sophisticated in her tailored designer duds and fancy handbag. No wonder she thought that Gabrielle looked frumpy in comparison in her gray pantsuit. "So how was the first half of your day?" Courtney inquired, peering down at her as she searched her purse for her keys. "I hope better than the first hour."

An image of Shane popped in Gabrielle's mind and she smiled warmly. "Much better. Mr. Adams and I are on the same page."

"I knew he'd come around," Courtney said as she walked toward the exit. Gabrielle assumed she was to follow and fell in beside her.

Once outside, Courtney stopped in front of the driver's side of her Porsche Boxster and quickly jumped in the convertible. "Well, don't just stand there. Get in!"

"Sorry," Gabrielle said as she slid into the passenger side. The seats were leather and felt as smooth as butter. "This is a nice ride."

"Thanks," Courtney responded as she fired up the engine. "Since it's your first day, I'm taking you to the Sun Dial." The trilevel restaurant inside the Westin Peachtree Plaza was known for having a spectacular view of the Atlanta skyline.

"Sounds great!" Gabrielle replied. "Doesn't it revolve?"

"How do you know? Are you from here?"

"Yes. I'm from Marietta."

"Really? Shane never told me you were from this area. Isn't it funny that you would both have careers in the same industry?"

Yeah, real funny, Gabrielle thought to herself. Courtney had no idea that she'd learned everything she knew from her father and Jax Cosmetics.

They arrived at the restaurant surprisingly quickly considering it was lunchtime. After a seventy-three-story elevator ride, the maître d' was waiting for them. He knew Courtney and seated them in a prime spot with a view of the CNN Center and the Georgia Dome. Gabrielle watched as he rushed to pull out Courtney's seat and saw how flustered he became when Courtney batted her eyelashes up at him. "Do men always treat you like that?" she inquired once they were seated and perusing the lunch menu.

"Like what?" Courtney asked.

"Never mind." Clearly Courtney was oblivious to the attention she obtained from the male species. Gabrielle doubted any man had ever looked at her quite like that. Not even Preston, with whom she'd shared a short but compatible relationship at school. He'd been a pleasant enough boyfriend who treated her well and who accepted her as she was. He hadn't expected her to gussy herself up.

"What are you having?" Courtney asked.

"Not sure yet."

"I'm thinking the flat-iron steak and mashed potatoes. Being a model is tough at times. I have to maintain my figure, otherwise I won't keep getting loaner clothes. So I'd better stick with the pecan-crusted chicken salad."

"That suit isn't yours?"

"No, the designers all send me clothes off the rack in the hopes that I will wear them and be photographed."

"It must be awful not to eat what you enjoy," Gabrielle said as she sipped on her water.

"That's the thing, I do eat," Courtney said, "which is why I'm in the gym six days a week, two hours a day to maintain this figure." She motioned down from her head to her toe. "Anyway, enough about me. Why don't you tell me the real reason you accepted a position with your archrival?"

Gabrielle nearly spit out her water and began coughing uncontrollably.

"I'm sorry," Courtney apologized and reached across to slap Gabrielle's back. "Are you okay?"

"Yes, I guess I wasn't prepared for you to be so…uh, straightforward."

Courtney smiled broadly. "You mean blunt, but I appreciate your tactfulness. You're also avoiding answering my question."

"Adams Cosmetics is a great company."

"But we are a small boutique firm," Courtney added.

"Not anymore."

"True." Courtney nodded. "But you must have known that accepting this position meant working closely with Shane, who according to him, you despised."

"Despise? No, I don't despise Shane," Gabrielle said. *How could she? She'd always been secretly attracted to him, but she would never tell another soul that.*

"Then what?"

"Then nothing." Gabrielle stared intently at the menu, hoping Courtney couldn't see the truth.

Courtney remained silent for several long, excruciating moments before finally saying, "You have a thing for my brother, don't you?"

"Shane?" Gabrielle's voice rose several octaves. "Of course not. We've always had a rivalry. Much like siblings would," she added for good measure, trying to cover her tracks.

"And you see my hazel-eyed, athletic, immensely attractive brother like a sibling?" Courtney raised a brow. *Now there was a lie she hadn't heard before.*

"I don't deny Shane has a certain *appeal*." Gabrielle chose her words very carefully. "He always has. I remember in school how he had a bevy of women who would fawn all over him, and he ate it up with a spoon. I'm sure Shane has never been at a loss for having a beautiful, sexy woman on his arm."

"Ah, so there's the rub," Courtney said, eyeing her suspiciously. "You're envious of the other women. You think he's superficial, so you've chosen to downplay your looks in the hopes that he will finally notice the inner you." Courtney placed her hand over Gabrielle's. "Darling, let me tell you, you could end up alone in bed every night if you continue on this route. There are a number of women trying to trap my brother into marriage, and if you don't act quickly, someone will snap him up."

"I am not interested in Shane."

"Sure, you're not."

The waiter came back to take their order and Courtney ordered the salad while Gabrielle chose the chicken fusilli pasta. That didn't prevent Courtney from taking up where she left off in the conversation once he'd gone. "My advice to you would be to glam it up. Let my brother see that you are a force to be reckoned with. And knowing Shane, he will not back down from a good challenge."

"How can you talk this way about your own brother?" Gabrielle asked Courtney. "You just met me, and clearly Shane did not speak well of me in the past."

"True, but I have a good feeling about you. I knew you were different when we met, which is why I asked you to lunch," Courtney replied. "Call it female intuition, but I think you are exactly what my brother needs."

"You have it all wrong, Courtney. I'm the exact opposite of the kind of woman your brother dates."

"Which is why you're absolutely perfect for him," Courtney replied. "And it's why I'm going to make you over so you can win him over."

Gabrielle sat in the car on the way back from lunch with Courtney completely flabbergasted. She'd tried explaining to Courtney that she dressed conservatively so that men would take her seriously in the lab. But the more she tried to convince Courtney that she wasn't interested in Shane, the more she dug in her heels, determined to fix the two of them up. Gabrielle could see the wheels turning in Courtney's mind.

She had to get her bearings at Adams Cosmetics first, and she couldn't afford a failed love affair with her boss. It had "disaster" written all over it. No, she had to make Courtney realize the error of her ways.

"Thank you again for lunch, Courtney," Gabrielle said as she exited the vehicle. "It was a really nice treat."

"You're absolutely welcome," Courtney answered. "I just know this is going to work out fine." She had barely finished her sentence when Shane pulled up beside her in his Jaguar.

Shane couldn't believe his eyes. Was that really his sister with Gabrielle Burton, of all people? Why was she being friendly with the enemy? He jumped out of the car with a frown on his face. "Courtney…" He nodded at his sister. "What's going on?"

Courtney looked at Shane then back at Gabrielle, trying to gauge their reaction to each other. "I ran into Gabby in the hall and took our new employee out for lunch. Do you have a problem with that?"

Gabrielle watched Shane's eyes narrow at Courtney's use of her nickname and her lack of response. Somehow Courtney using it didn't seem to bother her nearly as much as when Shane did.

"That's awfully nice of you, sister dear," Shane replied. "Remind me to thank you at dinner tonight. Gabrielle, if you're finished, can we get back to work?" Shane turned his back and headed into the building.

"Of course." Gabrielle smiled at Courtney before quickly rushing behind Shane. "See you soon." She waved to Courtney.

As he lay in bed, Shane stared at the ceiling and pondered how he was going to handle having Gabby in his domain. She was going to challenge him at every turn, just as she'd done in school, which had always been kind of a turn-on. Back then, he'd thought that all she needed was a good lay. You know, a man to work out all that inner hostility that she'd stored up and most often directed at him. And he'd thought that man might have been him, but Gabby had not been even remotely interested.

Shane had no idea why she'd taken such offense to him back then. Although they'd been rivals for the top spot, he'd always treated her with respect like the true southern boy he was, as his mother, Elizabeth, had raised him. Thinking about his mother brought a smile to his face. He'd inherited her easy nature, quick wit, fair coloring and beautiful hazel eyes, unlike Kayla, who had favored their father with his fiery temper and mahogany skin.

Although he loved his father, Shane had to admit Byron Adams was hard to handle and couldn't be an easy man to love, yet his mother made it look easy. He'd always wondered how his mother had endured thirty-five years of marriage, all the while helping Byron start his own cosmetics company.

His grandparents certainly hadn't been happy when she'd decided to end her three-year courtship with their choice for a mate, Andrew Jackson. He was born to the right family and had the right pedigree, unlike poor Byron Adams, a lowly employee of Graham International. They'd tried to talk her out of the marriage, but his mother loved his father, and although she hated to break Andrew's heart, she'd refused to give Byron up.

Elizabeth Adams was beautiful, intelligent, courageous and steadfastly loyal. Shane admired his mother a great deal, which is why few women could ever live up to his high standards. As he drifted off to sleep, Shane wondered if there was any woman who could.

In her hotel room later that evening, Gabrielle kicked off her heels and plopped down onto the plush pillow-top mattress. It was not going to be easy working with Shane day in and day out. He was conceited and superior, but despite those less-than-admirable qualities, she had to admit Shane was a brilliant and dedicated chemist. She was amazed at just how much he'd been overseeing in the laboratory.

He had projects in the works for every line of business at Adam Cosmetics. No wonder Ethan had looked at hiring him some help. If he continued at that pace, he would burn out. Of course, no one could tell him that. Like a typical male, Shane Adams was sure he could handle anything life threw at him.

But fortunately for him, she had some ideas of her own. She'd been cultivating them since she was at L'Oréal, but the head chemist had been unwilling to try them out. She hoped Shane wasn't as closed minded. She knew the lab was his domain, but she was determined to carve out a place for herself, even if it was by his side.

She was just about to head into the shower when she heard a knock on the door. Gabrielle had no idea who it could be, as she wasn't expecting anyone. Nothing could have shocked her further when she opened the door and saw the man standing on the other side was none other than Andrew Jackson.

Chapter 3

"Mr. Jackson?" Gabrielle gasped, touching her chest. "What are you doing here?" She hadn't seen her father's employer since she'd left Marietta well over eleven years ago. "And at this hour?"

Andrew Jackson looked the same as she remembered. He was well over six feet, lean and dark as night. Nearly a dozen years had passed, but he still wore his black hair the same, slicked back from his face without a hint of gray, and he had the same mysterious dark eyes. As a child, she could never tell if he was happy or sad.

"Gabrielle, how wonderful to see you again, darling," Andrew Jackson said with a country accent. He kissed her cheek and walked into her hotel room without an invitation.

Gabrielle was a little stunned at his rudeness, but closed the door anyway. *Did everyone think she was supposed to follow them today?* "I have to admit I'm surprised by the visit, Mr. Jackson."

"It has been a while, hasn't it?" Andrew glanced around the hotel room, noting the elegant decor and plush surroundings. Trust Ethan Graham to spare no expense when it came to hiring the best. He'd scouted a chemist last year himself, but had he known Gabrielle Burton was open to moving back to the States, he would have snapped her up himself. Jax Cosmetics could use a chemist like her.

He turned back around to face Gabrielle. "So, little lady, how has life been treating you in ole Paris? It's been what ten, eleven years since you've been home?"

"Give or take." Gabrielle had no intention of discussing her personal life with anyone, much less her father's employer.

"What can I do for you, Mr. Jackson? I'm sure you didn't come all this way to ask me about my years abroad."

Andrew laughed at Gabrielle's forthrightness. Time had turned the once-timid little girl into an outspoken woman. "I came by to bring you up to speed on what's been going on with your father."

"You're here about my father? Is something wrong? Is he okay?" Gabrielle's heart started pounding loudly in her chest. Although she may not be as close to her parents since Seth's death, she certainly didn't wish her father ill. And their family certainly couldn't handle another loss.

"No, no." Andrew took a seat on the couch. He spread his arm across the back and folded one leg across the other. "It's nothing like that."

Gabrielle preferred to stand while Andrew appeared to be making himself quite comfortable in her quarters. "Well, then, what is it?" What would bring Andrew Jackson all the way from Marietta to her hotel room at night uninvited?

"You may not be aware, but James has developed a drinking problem and a gambling habit."

Gabrielle folded her arms across her chest as she digested the information. For some reason, she wasn't surprised. Her father had always wanted more. A better house, a better job, more money, nicer clothes. It wasn't a stretch for her to imagine he thought he could win it at a casino table.

"He's racked up quite a debt," Andrew continued, watching Gabrielle carefully. She didn't bat an eyelash and appeared unaffected by the information he'd just given her. Perhaps he'd underestimated how far she would go to protect her family.

"What's it to you?" Gabrielle asked.

"To me?" Andrew asked. "I would imagine it would mean something to you since he's in debt to the wrong sort."

"And what do you mean by wrong sort?"

"The Goretti family," Andrew answered swiftly. "You may not have heard of them, but they are the sort who don't mind breaking a few ribs, if you get my drift."

"I do. But if the 'wrong sort'—" Gabrielle used her hands to make quotation marks "—are looking for money, they are barking up the wrong tree. I live within my means."

Andrew raised a brow. "You don't sugarcoat your words, young lady, so let me get straight to the point. I would be willing to pay your father's debt, if you do something for me in return."

"Of course." Gabrielle laughed shrilly as understanding dawned on her. "You wouldn't help him altruistically."

They had come to the crux of why Andrew Jackson was there in the first place. He wanted something from her. What? She wasn't sure. She couldn't fathom what she could possibly offer him that was worthwhile. She had some money in savings for a rainy day, but that was about it. "What do you want, Mr. Jackson?"

A crooked smile spread across Andrew's face. "I hear you've accepted a position with Adams Cosmetics. And that could be beneficial to me."

Gabrielle frowned and several lines formed across her forehead. "I don't understand. How so?"

Andrew couldn't believe how naive Gabrielle was. He would have to spell it out. "You could supply me with information."

"What kind of information?"

"Oh, you know…" He paused. "Their latest research, marketing and, of course, any upcoming products." Andrew searched her face to ensure she was getting exactly what was on the table.

"You want me to commit corporate espionage?" Gabrielle couldn't believe her ears.

"I wouldn't call it that," Andrew said. "I would say one hand is washing another. You give me information to help boost Jax Cosmetics and help level the playing field. In return, I save your father from a terrible fate at the hands of some mob henchmen."

Gabrielle swallowed hard. There was a reason she had never quite trusted Andrew Jackson even as a child, and now she knew why. He was the devil incarnate.

"I think you should go, Mr. Jackson." Gabrielle had heard enough and walked toward the door.

Slowly, Andrew rose to his feet, buttoned his suit jacket. He walked toward her and when he reached her, he glared down at her. "Listen, little girl, your father is in a bind."

Gabrielle hated his condescending word usage, but couldn't help replying much too petulantly to her liking, "My *father* is a grown man. He made his bed and he'll have to lie in it."

"So you would leave your father hanging in the wind?" Andrew asked. When she didn't answer right away, Andrew knew there was still hope he could get her to do his bidding. "Why don't you take a little time to think about it?" He opened the door to her suite. "I'll be back in touch."

Seconds later, the door closed behind him, and Gabrielle breathed a sigh of relief. *What the hell had just happened? Had Andrew Jackson really just asked her to risk her job, her freedom and commit corporate espionage to save a father who in the past decade hadn't shown an ounce of interest in her?*

"Morning," Shane said unenthusiastically at the breakfast table the next morning. It was a beautiful day, and their butler had set up a table out on the terrace so they could enjoy the fresh air.

"Hello, grumpy," Courtney said as she poured granola over her fruit yogurt. She'd just enjoyed a leisurely dip in the pool and was famished.

"I'm not in the mood for you today, Courtney." He'd slept fitfully the night before, barely getting a few hours of sleep, and now he was irritable. He reached for the carafe of coffee and poured a cup. He drank it black, uncharacteristically.

"Okay, okay." Courtney held up her hands. "I will leave you alone." She ran her fingers through her damp hair.

"What has got you in a bad mood?" his mother asked, sipping her coffee. It wasn't like her son to be so snippy with his sister.

"No reason." Shane lowered his head, adding some eggs and bacon to his plate from a nearby platter.

"Are you sure about that?" Elizabeth looked at her son suspiciously. She could read him and knew when he was hiding something. "How did it go with your new employee yesterday? You weren't at dinner last night, so I couldn't ask you how it went."

"It went fine." Shane dug his fork into his eggs and ate a generous amount.

"You could have fooled me," Courtney returned. "I ran into her in the hall and she looked positively flustered."

"Puh-lease," Shane responded, taking a bite of bacon. "Gabrielle Burton can hold her own. She gave as good as she got."

"But you were professional?" his mother countered.

"Of course, Mom. Courtney here even took her out for lunch on her first day."

"That was kind of you," their mother replied, turning to her daughter. "Is she as bad as Shane says?"

"No," Courtney said, glaring at Shane. "She's a lovely woman, though she could use a little fixing up. I told her I would help her."

"So she's your new pet project?" Shane inquired, raising an eyebrow. "I believe you have better and more important things to do with your time at Adams Cosmetics than fix up some straightlaced prude."

"Shane!" Elizabeth was flabbergasted at her son's response.

"See, I told you, Mama." Courtney pointed at Shane. "He has it out for her. He wants her to fail." For some reason, she felt as if she had to fight for Gabby, maybe because she was the only woman who'd ever gotten under her brother's skin.

"I do not have it out for her," Shane replied testily. "Nothing I've said isn't the truth. You know as well as I do that Gabrielle Burton could stand to loosen up a bit."

"But there's no reason to be mean," their mother admonished. "That is no way to treat a lady. I'm warning you, Shane. I better not hear that you've mistreated the young woman."

Shane rolled his eyes at his younger sister. He didn't appreciate a scolding by his mother. He was a grown man, after all. "If you'll excuse me." He scooted back from the table, nearly knocking his chair over. "I wouldn't want to burden you with my presence." He walked off the terrace and headed toward the front of the house, where he'd parked his Jaguar.

When he arrived at the laboratory, he was in no better of a mood. Gabrielle must have sensed his inner turmoil, because she gave him a wide berth that morning. She chose instead to work with several other members of his staff, and that was just fine with him. Shane didn't know why her presence bothered him, but bothered he was. Even more so when he saw her dressed in a prim black skirt with a white silk blouse that tied at the neck. He wanted nothing more than to untie that knot and free her of her inhibitions.

Shane shook his head. *Where the hell had that thought come from?* He turned around and glanced in her direction. Gabrielle must have sensed it because she looked up at him with her almond-shaped eyes and gave him a broad smile. He noticed that she was wearing her hair differently from yesterday's prim look. Instead of having her hair in an updo, she'd decided for a half up, half down look.

He looked away and returned his focus to his perfumer's organ and pulled out several scents. He was determined to hit the right notes today and get this fragrance right, once and for all.

From the other side of the lab, Gabrielle reengaged herself with her coworker on the new skin-care products in development. She hadn't meant to smile at Shane, but when she'd found him staring at her so openly, she'd thought they were off to a new start. She must have been wrong, because he hadn't returned the smile; he'd ignored her and looked down.

She didn't know why she was thinking about him anyway. She had more important things to worry about. Namely, Andrew Jackson. Overnight, she'd had to time to think, and thanks to Jackson, she felt compelled to at least reach out to her father and find out exactly what was going on. She didn't relish the task. She hadn't spoken more than polite pleasantries to her parents in over a decade.

She wasn't sure if they even wanted to see her. If she didn't call them, they certainly didn't call her. Ever since Seth's death, it was as if she didn't exist. It hurt knowing they didn't even think about her, but she'd had to make her peace with being alone in the world.

After much debate, Gabrielle decided to call her parents when lunchtime came around. She left the laboratory and walked outside to the courtyard, where most folks were congregated for lunch. It was a beautifully manicured garden. Gabrielle dialed her parents' number and waited with bated breath for someone to answer. She was hoping no one was home and that she could just leave a message and walk away unscathed.

No such luck. Her mother picked up on the third ring. "Hello."

"Hi, Mom, it's Gabrielle." She took a seat on a nearby concrete bench.

"Gabby?" her mother asked. "What are you doing calling during the middle of the day? Are you in some kind of trouble?"

"Trouble?" It was more the other way around. Though Gabrielle doubted her mother knew a thing about her father's gambling habit. "No, of course not. I'm here in the States. Georgia, to be exact." Her words nearly jumbled together as she tried to get them all out.

"Well, that's good to hear," her mother replied. "You should come home and get some real food instead of all that French cooking."

Actually, Gabrielle had become accustomed to French cooking and quite enjoyed it, but that was another matter entirely. "That would be nice," Gabrielle said, using it as an opening. "I was actually hoping I could stop by this Sunday for a visit, if that's all right."

"We have plans this week," her mother responded, "How about next Sunday? I can make your favorite dish, shepherd's pie."

Tears formed in Gabrielle's eyes. She was surprised her mother even remembered what she liked. "Th-That would be great." Gabrielle choked the words out. Although she wanted to talk to her father sooner, she would have to wait. Andrew Jackson hadn't given her a time constraint.

"We'll see you Sunday at three, right after church."

"See you then." Gabrielle ended the call as fresh tears surfaced on her cheeks. *How could one phone call from her mother make her come apart?* She was so wrapped up in her own thoughts that she didn't hear Shane come up beside her.

Shane bent down until he was eye to eye with Gabrielle. "Are you okay?"

Gabrielle turned away and swiftly began wiping away the tears with the back of her hand. She didn't want him to see her like this.

"Gabrielle," he said more sternly, grabbing both her shoulders and turning her around to face him. "What's wrong? Did something happen?" He'd never seen her so, so…vulnerable, and it called out to every male instinct in him to protect her.

"Everything is fine." She kept her head low, but Shane lifted her chin with his hand.

"Everything is far from fine," he said, peering into her eyes. "Whoever it was on the other end of that call obviously upset you a great deal. Is there anything I can do?"

His burning eyes held her. She couldn't believe Shane was being so nice to her. Where was the arrogant, cocky man she was used to?

Shane reached in his suit pocket and handed her a handkerchief and then scooted himself next to her on the bench. That tiny act of kindness had Gabrielle questioning everything she'd ever thought about Shane. She accepted the handkerchief and used it to wipe her eyes, blow her nose and get control of her emotions.

"Feel better?" Shane asked, pushing her hair back so he could see her face. Her skin was bright, nearly translucent. Seeing Gabby in this light, so vulnerable, made her seem more human and attractive, which surprisingly had his groin tightening in response. *What was wrong with him? This was Gabby Burton, Gabrielle Burton, the hard-nosed chemist who'd been driven to beat him at all costs in perfumery school. So why was he finding himself wondering what lay beneath that cool reserve of hers?*

Gabrielle's mouth curved into a smile, and Shane found his heart beating just a little bit faster. "Yes, much."

"Good. So what do you say we go back inside and get back to work?" Shane asked.

"Sounds good."

The rest of the afternoon went by quickly, as did the remainder of the week. Gabrielle found herself enjoying her position immensely. She'd even offered her opinion to Shane about what chemical to put in the new skin-care lotion, and he hadn't bitten her head off. They were definitely making progress. She'd caught him staring at her again several times, but he'd looked away, as if his hand had been caught in the cookie jar.

She was so deep in work on one formula on Friday evening that the time got away from her, and when she glanced up, she noticed that only she and Shane were still in the lab. She glanced at her watch and realized it was nearly 7:00 p.m., way past quitting time. She walked over to Shane and leaned over his shoulder to see what he was working on.

The scent of Gabrielle wafted to Shane's nose. It wasn't the scent of any perfume, because his nose didn't detect any notes. It was her natural smell. Not to mention he could feel her warmth from behind him. He spun around on his stool. "You ready to get out of here?" he asked, surprising himself. "We could grab a cocktail, and you could finally let your hair down for a change." He could use a drink; he was wound up too tight.

"After that flattering invitation, how can I turn you down?" Gabrielle asked curtly. "And if you hadn't noticed, my hair is down."

"Oh, c'mon, Gabby." Shane continued to call her by her nickname. "I was just razzing you. Don't tell me you can't take the heat? I remember you dishing it out in school rather well." He recalled how she'd once called him an egotistical spoiled rich boy.

"I can take the heat!" Gabrielle huffed. "I'll just get my suit jacket."

"Leave it!" Shane ordered before she could make a move. He went to the laboratory door and held it open. "You could stand to loosen up a bit and go with a more casual look."

Gabrielle's cheeks burned fire as she walked toward him. "Oh, I will show you I can loosen up. Just you wait."

"Bring it on, Gabby," Shane said as he followed her through the double doors. He was eager to finally see her look less like a schoolmarm and more like a woman.

The jazz lounge Shane took her to was filled with the after-work set wanting to ease the load after a hard day. Gabrielle could sure use a drink. The phone call with her mother a few days ago had released some emotions she'd thought she'd buried. She'd thought she was long past caring if her parents wanted to see her, so it had surprised her when her mother remembered her favorite meal.

Shane, meanwhile, was uneasy. He'd been feeling off-kilter all day and was happy when Gabrielle had insisted on driving separately in her rental car. It gave him some breathing room and time to figure out what it was he was doing. He'd never dated a coworker, much less a subordinate. Though cocktails after work hardly qualified as a date, he would never have thought he would willingly spend time in Gabrielle Burton's company. Yet there was something about her that intrigued him. He wanted to know more.

They slid inside a plush velvet booth and a blonde waitress in an electric-blue bustier came over to ask for their drink order. She was buxom, just how he liked his women; he couldn't even tell if Gabrielle had a figure under the dour clothes she wore. "We'll have two Scorpions."

Gabrielle huffed from his side. "Do you always order for your women? Because I'm quite capable of doing so myself."

Shane smiled at her Miss Independent stance. "It *is* their signature drink. Trust me, you'll love it. It has bite."

"Well apparently, I'll have to love it."

"Must you always be so…so obstinate?"

His word choice made Gabrielle laugh. No one had ever used that adjective to describe her before. "Only with you," she added.

Shane turned to face her. "Why is that? Why do I seem to irk you so much?"

Gabrielle cocked her head to one side. "Honestly?"

"Honesty would be nice."

"In school, it was because you were a privileged playboy who didn't have to work hard like the rest of us."

"How the hell do you think I got in? They only took the best."

"Back then, I thought you'd bought your way in," Gabrielle replied. "But then I soon realized you had talent to back up all that bravado, and I had some competition. I didn't like it."

"No, you didn't."

The waitress came back with their drinks and Shane lifted his glass. "Welcome aboard, Gabby."

Gabrielle sighed. It was clear that Shane wasn't going to stop calling her by her nickname. But she supposed it wasn't so bad after all. "Thank you." She lifted her glass and clicked it against his.

"I have to ask, what made you decide to leave L'Oréal to come to a lesser-known company?" Shane inquired, sipping his drink. "Most chemists would have thought that a dream job."

"And initially it was," Gabrielle replied. "When you're a young chemist you see stars, but as time passed it became harder and harder to make my mark."

"And you see that chance here at Adams Cosmetics, I surmise?"

"If you're willing to hear what I have to say, I can."

Gabrielle took a liberal sip of her drink. "Mmm… This is good."

"Told ya." Shane grinned. "So you're not sure if I'll listen to what you have to say?" He responded to her former comment.

"Well…" Gabrielle shrugged. "You have made it clear that the laboratory is your area and that you have to approve everything." She hazarded a look at him. "An Adams will always run Adams Cosmetics," she said, attempting to sound masculine.

Shane leaned back and laughed heartily. "That was a pretty good imitation. You see, Adams Cosmetics is not just a company to me—it's my family's business. It's my heritage. It's what I will leave behind to my kids. The same as my dad did for me and my sisters. I'm sorry if I sounded territorial."

The passion with which Shane spoke about AC had Gabrielle realizing she had misjudged him. There was truly depth of character to him. He wasn't just some spoiled rich boy.

"But I promise you this," Shane continued. "If you bring me a solid idea that will improve the products we're producing, I will listen. Fair enough?"

Shane smiled back at her, and Gabrielle's insides turned to mush. There was no other way to describe the feeling, but at that exact moment, she became smitten with Shane Adams. Now she could see why women lined up to spend time with him. He had such a subtle way of charming a woman's socks off that she didn't realize she'd been charmed until the damage was done. "Fair enough," she finally said, putting down her drink.

"Good, I'm glad that's settled," Shane said. "So if we're going to spend time together, I'd like to know more about you."

"What do you want to know?"

"For one, why did you decide to stay in Paris after school?"

"At the time L'Oréal seemed like a dream job, and I didn't particularly want to come home."

"Why not? Is there bad blood between you and your family?"

"I guess you could say that."

"Where are you from, if you don't mind my asking?"

"Actually, here in Georgia. Marietta, to be exact."

"Really?" Shane was surprised. He'd always taken her for an East Coast girl who went to some preppy boarding school, which was why she acted so prim and proper. "And what made you decide on perfumery school of all places? Paris is a long way from Marietta." He'd noticed Gabrielle was fidgeting in the booth, as if the topic of her past made her uncomfortable.

"I'd always enjoyed chemistry and how things were made. Just seemed like a natural progression."

"I beg to differ. For me, yes. My family owns a cosmetics company, but you, you don't even wear makeup. And well, perfume, you're not wearing any."

"Wow, you don't miss much." She'd never quite mastered the art of putting on makeup. In Paris, she'd been too embarrassed to ask one of the makeup artists to teach her, so outside of a quick glide of lip gloss, she didn't wear any.

"I am in the beauty business. And I know women," Shane said.

"Oh, I know."

"You make it sound like a bad thing," Shane replied, watching her carefully. "I happen to enjoy beautiful women and appreciate the female form. There is nothing wrong with that."

"I never said there was."

"No, you just implied it," Shane responded. He leaned forward until he was inches away from her face. He stared deep into her big brown eyes. "Do you even know how to have fun? You know, let go."

Shane was so close to her, he could almost kiss her. *Where had that thought come from? She didn't want him to kiss her. Or so she told herself. It was just hard not to notice the raw masculinity and sexual energy radiating out of his every pore.* Gabrielle pushed away from the table. "Of course. In Paris I spent time with my friends at the art galleries…museums…cafés. It was quite brilliant, I'll have you know."

"It sounds *brilliant,*" Shane imitated her. "But I wasn't talking about your friends. I was talking about with a man."

Gabrielle watched as Shane's large masculine fingers rimmed the top of his glass. When his finger dipped inside to taste the drink and he licked it off, she swallowed hard. He couldn't know how sexy that little action was to her. She could feel her body temperature rising, and she began to feel warm all over. Or perhaps it was just the way Shane was looking at her. It was the first time she'd seen him look at her that way. He wasn't looking at her as a co-worker or former rival. He was looking at her as a woman.

"I…I've had boyfriends."

Shane raised an eyebrow in amusement. "You mean Preston?" He couldn't resist a chuckle.

"Why are you laughing?"

"Because I doubt Preston knew what to do with a woman, much less a woman as independent and *obstinate* as you. You probably walked all over the poor schmuck. I doubt that was much of a turn-on. No woman likes a man she can walk over."

"Excuse me? You have no idea what I like *or* what turns me on."

"Wanna bet?" Shane took her statement as a challenge and rose from the booth.

"What are you doing?" She looked up at him.

"Let's dance." Shane didn't wait for her to answer. Instead, he placed his empty glass on the table, and pulled her out of the booth and toward the dance floor.

Gabrielle tried unsuccessfully to pull away. "I can't dance. I have two left feet."

"Don't worry. I'll lead you," Shane said. When Gabrielle hesitated, he asked, "I thought you said you could take the heat?"

"I *can,*" Gabrielle said more firmly, in an attempt to convince herself. "I can take the heat." Her head was spinning at being this close to Shane and she felt rattled. She'd always thought he was attractive. Who wouldn't? But this, this was different. This was deeper and coming from a place more primal. She wanted him.

Shane grasped one of her hands in his and placed the other around his waist. Then he twirled her onto the dance floor and circled his arm around her waist.

Gabrielle was breathless and just a tad bit giddy as they danced. Shane guided her easily around the dance floor to the midtempo jazz tune. He bent down to rest his head lightly against the side of her face, and she could feel his breath against her cheek.

A slow song came on and Shane slowed the tempo. Shane closed the gap between them until they were chest to chest and hip to hip. When he ground his hips against hers, Gabrielle thought she might faint. Her cheeks became warm, and she could feel liquid heat, unlike any she'd ever felt before, pooling in the lower half of her body. There was no mistaking that Shane Adams knew *exactly* what turned her on.

And when his hands reached out to caress her face, Gabrielle couldn't help but look up into his hazel eyes. She understood what she saw there: lust, plain and simple. But she never expected him to act on it. So she was surprised when Shane leaned down to brush his lips gently across hers. It was the softest of kisses, but it sent a shiver running up her spine all the same. She didn't—couldn't—stop him when he deepened the kiss.

Shane was happy Gabrielle didn't stop the kiss, because it allowed his tongue entry into her hot, waiting mouth. She tasted juicy and sweet, like nectar, and Shane wanted more. He pulled her more firmly to him, fusing their mouths and tongues together. He was just about to suck on her tongue, when the music stopped.

Shane pulled up, and Gabrielle opened her eyes at the sudden interruption of something she wasn't even sure she'd wanted until now.

Shane stepped away from her, running his fingers through his curly fro. "That shouldn't have happened." Disappointment showed in Gabrielle's eyes at his comment, but he couldn't help it. Gabrielle wasn't even his type, so he didn't know why he was mauling her on the dance floor in front of witnesses. Worse yet, she was his employee. "We should go." He motioned for her to precede him off the dance floor.

When they returned to the table, Gabrielle's head was hung low, as if she was embarrassed. But he was the one who'd kissed her. "Listen, Gabby," Shane began, but she held up her hand.

"Don't bother to explain," Gabrielle replied. "I understand. I know it was an impulsive move. I mean…I'm not even your type, right?" She laughed nervously. "I'm not beautiful or glamorous like the women you're used to. I'm just plain old Gabby. I mean, who would want to kiss me?" Gabrielle stood suddenly, reached for her purse on the table and quickly rushed out of the lounge.

Chapter 4

Shane noticed that Gabrielle maintained her distance the following week. She spoke when spoken to, but there was no friendly conversation as there had been during her first week. And when lunchtime came around, she bolted out of the room so fast he had no time to speak to her about what had happened that night at the lounge.

She wasn't the only one stunned by that kiss; Shane had been surprised too by the attraction he'd felt for Gabby. Matter of fact, if the music hadn't stopped, he would have continued kissing her, fueled by the lower half of his body. Gabrielle was right when she said she was normally not his type, but she was wrong if she thought he'd pulled away because she wasn't beautiful enough. Gabrielle had a natural soft beauty of her own; she had warm almond-shaped brown eyes, a perky nose, round cheeks and clear skin, all without the benefit of makeup. She was beautiful in her own right. And he was sorry if he'd made her feel otherwise.

And he would tell her all of that if she would give him half a chance, but she seemed determined not to speak to him. She'd done everything she could to keep him at arm's length, and it frustrated the hell out of him.

When the end of the day came, Gabrielle was the first one to leave, barely saying goodbye as she left. Perhaps Gabby was on to something. Maybe it was better if they kept their relationship strictly business.

Gabrielle exhaled once she'd finally gotten in her rental car and started the engine. She'd done a good job of dodging Shane the past week and had avoided having an embarrassing conversation about how he regretted the kiss, which just so happened to be *the best kiss* she'd ever had. It was passion and lust all rolled into one, and she'd wanted it to continue, but obviously Shane hadn't. He probably preferred his women to be beautiful, sexy and voluptuous, which she wasn't. She had slender hips, B-cup-size breasts and a small behind.

Maybe Courtney had been on to something when she'd indicated Gabrielle could use a makeover. If she appealed to Shane's male sensibilities and his appreciation of the female form, perhaps then he would listen to her ideas. She could use her womanly charms to make him cooperate with her in the lab. *Should she take Courtney up on her offer?* And if she did, would Shane then notice her and realize she could be sexy and worthy of his attention?

Gabrielle couldn't believe she was actually considering changing her appearance. She told herself it was to make headway in her profession and it wasn't for a man, but deep down she knew it was. She wanted Shane to find her desirable, because as much as she tried to hide it, tried to ignore it, the attraction she'd once felt for Shane was still there.

* * *

"Pull!" Shane ordered Victor, their butler, on Saturday morning from outside the family estate as he aimed the double-barreled shotgun in the air at the clay pigeon. Victor was operating the target thrower that morning so Shane could relieve some tension.

The clay pigeon went flying into the air and Shane tracked it with a steady, smooth swing. Once he had a good eye on the disk's trajectory, he pulled the trigger and fired.

Bam. He hit it dead center.

Shane moved to a different angle and made an adjustment to his position. "Pull!"

He continued the exercise at least a dozen times before stopping to rest. Shane was walking back to get a cool drink when he noticed Kayla standing beside Victor, holding out a bottle of water for him.

He handed the shotgun to Victor before accepting the bottle. "Thanks." He twisted off the cap and drank liberally.

"Have a little aggression you need to get out?" Kayla inquired, rubbing her steadily increasing belly.

"Why would you say that?" Shane asked, leaning back to take another swig of water.

"Hmm…" Kayla shrugged. "I don't know, perhaps because skeet shooting is a somewhat aggressive sport."

"It's not like I'm killing birds or something," Shane snapped.

Kayla smiled despite his tone. "No, but there's obviously something on your mind." She and Shane were close, and she could read him just as he could read her. "Care to tell me about it?"

"Not particularly."

Kayla's eyes narrowed. Shane was more guarded than

usual, which meant this was about a woman. He became quiet and withdrawn only when it came to his private life.

"What?" He hated that Kayla was staring at him, trying to figure him out.

"You might as well tell me, because you know I'm like a pit bull."

"Walk with me," Shane said, entwining his arm with hers and walking back toward the house. He turned back momentarily. "Victor, I'm done for now. Thank you."

"So…" Kayla bumped her shoulder against his forearm. "What's going on? I hope this isn't about Gabrielle Burton."

"In a way it sort of is."

"I thought after our talk on her first day that you guys were getting along," Kayla said. She hadn't heard a peep out of Shane all week, so she'd assumed the situation was handled.

"It's not about that," Shane said.

"Then what?"

Shane stopped in his tracks and regarded her sideways. "Who am I talking to now?" he asked. "Am I talking to my sister and confidante, or am I talking to the president of Adams Cosmetics?"

Kayla paused. "I don't think I know how to differentiate." Adams Cosmetics was a part of her just as much as it was a part of Shane.

Shane raised an eyebrow and became silent.

Kayla got the message. "Okay…okay. You're talking to your sister. So what happened?"

"I kissed Gabrielle," Shane blurted out.

"You did *what?*" Kayla stopped in her tracks.

Shane pointed a finger at her. "You promised me you were going to listen as *my sister.*"

Kayla inhaled deeply and started walking again.

"You're right. I'm sorry. But how could this have happened? I thought you didn't like Gabrielle Burton."

"I don't. Or I *didn't*," he corrected himself. "But something changed." Shane opened the terrace door so Kayla could enter the mansion.

"Clearly."

"Kayla…" Shane warned and pulled her into the study so no one in the family could hear their conversation. "Don't you think this is upsetting to me, too? I mean, one minute I'm against hiring her, and the next she's in my arms on the dance floor. Then one thing…just led to another."

Kayla laughed at Shane's interpretation of events. She doubted it was as simple as that. "And how did you end up dancing?" she asked, sitting down in a nearby chair. She needed to get off her feet. Standing for long periods was becoming increasingly difficult.

"We decided to go out after work for an innocent cocktail," Shane said. "I was trying to be friendly. I thought it might be nice to blow off some steam."

"And instead you ended up kissing?" Kayla smiled. "Hmm…"

"What does that 'hmm' mean?" Shane asked, looking down at her. "I didn't want it to happen."

"Who are you trying to convince? Me or yourself?" Shane didn't answer, so Kayla continued, "Deep down on some level, despite your protests to the contrary, you are attracted to plain ole Gabrielle."

"She's not plain!"

Kayla held up her hands to defend herself. "Whoa! I was merely using the words *you'd* used to describe her once, but I can see you feel differently now."

Shane shook his head. "I guess I do. Up until now, we'd never really spent a significant amount of time together, so perhaps I didn't really know her when I formed that opinion."

"Sounds very logical."

Shane glanced sideways at Kayla. "Why do I hear a hint of sarcasm in your voice?"

"Because everything you're saying makes sense," Kayla said. "I'm just curious how you're going to handle your feelings for Gabrielle going forward."

"I'm not."

"You're such a man!" Kayla sighed. "You think you can just ignore them?"

"That's exactly what I'm going to do," Shane replied huffily. "You know as well as I do that the kiss should never have happened. Gabby is my employee, and although she may not be plain, she really isn't my type. I must have gotten caught up in the moment. And Gabby obviously feels the way or she wouldn't be ignoring me now."

Kayla shrugged. "Is that what has you out of sorts? That she's ignoring you? It's probably her defense mechanism. And you may recall I tried to ignore my feelings for Ethan, too, and I didn't fare too well in that department."

"That was different. You had a crush on him since you were a little girl," Shane said. "I, on the other hand, have *never* thought of Gabby in a romantic light."

"Fine. It's your life." Kayla shrugged. "I'm just telling you, I learned a thing or two when I fell for Ethan. And the heart wants what it wants."

Shane shook his head. Kayla was wrong. He knew what he wanted, and it was not Gabrielle Burton.

"I'm ready," Gabrielle told Courtney later that morning after they'd just finished a Pilates class at Courtney's country club. Courtney had contacted her the previous evening and invited her. Now they were in the steam room, sweating in the heat that had risen to nearly one hundred degrees after Courtney had thrown some additional water on the stones.

"Ready for what?" Courtney asked from her position laid out on one of the sauna benches. She was lost in the haze of smoke.

"For a makeover."

That perked Courtney up. She jumped to sit upright and faced Gabrielle on the opposite side of the sauna. "Really? You're willing to let me make you over from head to toe?"

"Yes."

Courtney's eyes narrowed, and she tried to figure out Gabrielle. "Why the change of heart? I thought you were dead set against it. I thought you were happy with the way you look."

"It's just time for a change," Gabrielle replied. "I'm back in the States with a new job and I want to command attention, so I need a new look. You know, new hairdo, new clothes…the works."

"Oh…" Courtney rubbed her hands together in glee. "This is going to be so much fun. You'll see. You won't know what to do with all the attention you'll get once I'm done with you. The men will be lined up at your door."

"Sounds great." Gabrielle smiled, but the only man she truly wanted to notice her was Shane. She just hoped that once he saw her, he would no longer see a frog, but a princess whom he wouldn't mind kissing.

"How about we shoot for next Saturday?" Courtney asked. "My family is having a dinner party at the estate and we're inviting a few friends. You should come. It would be a great opportunity to show off your new look."

"You're on." Gabrielle leaned over to shake her hand.

* * *

As she drove to her parents' home later on Sunday afternoon, Gabrielle wondered what Shane was up to. Focusing on something else was better than the alternative, which was worrying about visiting her parents, whom she hadn't seen in over a decade. *Had they even wondered how she was at times? If she was dead or alive?*

If they did, she would have never known because they'd never tried to call, much less visit her in Paris. Most parents would jump at the chance to visit their daughter in Paris and not have to worry about lodging, but when she'd suggested a visit, they'd made up excuses. Her father couldn't get the time off work, or her mother hated flying long distances. *Since when?* They'd driven most places for family trips when Seth was alive. How did her mother know she didn't like flying?

Seth. Her dear brother. Taken from them too young. To this day, Gabrielle could remember him helping her up into the boat after a storm had come suddenly and a wave had knocked her overboard. Being her big brother, he'd dived in after her and gotten her to safety, but then another wave had hit, throwing him backward into the water. She could still remember his friends' screams as the thunder and roaring waves got louder, and Seth drifted farther and farther out to sea. They'd tried to paddle toward him, but the current was too strong.

Why was it that just thinking about spending time with her parents caused her to relive Seth's drowning? She'd thought, or hoped, that time would heal the wounds, but they seemed just as raw as ever. Even more so when her rental car pulled into the driveway of her parents' home and it was the same as she remembered the day she left, except maybe with a fresher coat of paint. The lawn was still beautifully manicured, and her mother's rocker still sat outside on the porch by her geraniums.

Was she ready to face them after all this time? She didn't have time to find out, because the front door opened and her mother came out to greet her. *Now that was a surprise.*

Slowly, Gabrielle exited the vehicle and swung her purse over her shoulder.

"Gabby," her mother said as she waved from the porch. "C'mon inside. I have some sweet tea waiting for you."

"Uh…thanks," Gabrielle said, walking up the wooden steps. It felt as if she was going to the gauntlet. "You shouldn't have."

"Oh, shush, it was no trouble," her mother said.

When she made it to the top, instead of enveloping her in a warm hug after a decade apart, her mother gave her a quick pat on the back and walked inside their family home. Gabrielle didn't know why she'd expected anything different, but she had. She'd hoped that time had lessened the pain for her mother and helped her finally acknowledge that she still had one child left. *She was wrong.*

"Your father isn't home yet," her mother was saying as Gabrielle walked into the foyer. "But I'm sure he'll be back for dinner."

He was *exactly* the person she needed to speak with to find out if what Andrew Jackson had said was true, but it appeared she would have to bide her time.

"Don't just stand there," her mother said. "Come into the parlor." She gestured for Gabrielle to follow her.

Once inside, a pitcher of sweet iced tea and tea biscuits awaited Gabrielle. Her mother still remembered that the tea biscuits, which were more like rich butter cookies, were her favorites. Some were plain and others were topped with milk chocolate, but Gabrielle liked them all the same.

Gabby took a seat across from her mother while she poured her a glass of iced tea and set about making her a small plate. She had forgotten how Southern her mother truly was. Time had weathered Pamela Burton's face, and there were more lines than Gabrielle remembered. She'd put on a few extra pounds, but generally speaking her mother looked in good health. It was a small consolation, but she could be happy about that.

"Thank you." Gabrielle accepted the plate and immediately began munching on the cookies. She could never resist them when she was a little girl.

"Slow down, there's more in the kitchen." Her mother pointed in that direction. "I made a tin that you can take with you."

"That's very kind of you."

"So." Her mother leaned back in her chair and assessed her. "You're looking well if not a little thin, dear."

"Thanks, I think."

"You'll never meet and marry a man if you don't have some meat on your bones."

If putting some meat on her bones was the way to win Shane's attention, she'd readily do it, but she doubted that was it. Shane Adams didn't see her as beautiful *or* sexy. He thought she was a "Plain Jane," but Gabrielle intended to change all that. After Courtney's makeover, he would think she was as beautiful and sophisticated as any woman he'd ever dated.

"By the way, are you seeing anyone?" her mother inquired.

Why did she have to ask the dreaded question that every single woman hated to be asked? "Not at *the moment*."

"But you have someone in mind?" Her mother picked up on the inflection in her tone.

"Perhaps, but it's too soon to say. Time will tell." Gabrielle couldn't believe they were having a normal mother-daughter conversation.

"I'm so happy to hear that," her mother said. "There's nothing worse than being alone."

And then she went and blew it. "Being alone has its advantages," Gabrielle responded.

"Like what?" her mother asked as if she really couldn't fathom how any woman would enjoy the prospect.

"You can come and go as you please," Gabrielle offered. "You have no one to answer to."

"But no one who cares about you."

"That wouldn't be any different for me," Gabrielle said. The moment the words were out of her mouth, she wished she could take them back.

"You don't think you have anyone who cares about you?" Her mother seemed genuinely surprised by her statement.

Gabrielle was tongue-tied. Here was the opportunity to put her cards out on the table. Finally get it out in the open that she'd felt like an afterthought once Seth was gone, but she heard the front door close and soon her father was standing in front of her in the parlor.

"Gabrielle." He nodded in her direction. "Pamela, fix me a drink, would ya?" he ordered as he plopped down in the recliner opposite Gabrielle.

Her mother quickly got up and rushed to the small bar in the room to make him a drink. Gabrielle remembered her dad having a drink every now and again, but since when was he a heavy drinker? Apparently, Andrew Jackson was right about something.

Gabrielle was shocked at the appearance of the man sitting before her. Gone was the fun-loving, kind, compassionate father who used to sneak her and Seth into the Jax Cosmetics lab. In his place was a cold, stone-faced man with a weathered look on his face and a mess of silver hair. *What had happened to her father? When had he turned into a ghost of his former self? Had her leaving nearly a decade ago done this? Would staying have helped?*

As she stared back at him, she doubted it. Staying would have only hardened her and made her hate her parents. "Daddy, it's good to see you."

"Wish I could say the same," he huffed as he gulped down half the drink her mother had handed him.

"James!"

"Pamela, we haven't seen this girl in ten, twelve years, and now I hear she's accepted a job at Adams Cosmetics?" Her father's voice rose as he spoke. "I mean, where's the loyalty—after everything Andrew Jackson has done for this family."

Anger boiled inside Gabrielle. If he thought she would just sit back and be attacked, he had another thought coming. "*I* owe Andrew Jackson nothing."

"Is that right?" Her father's eyes narrowed as they washed over her. "It's because of him that I kept food on the table and clothes on your back! Pamela, I need another drink!"

Her mother jumped up from her chair to get him another.

"*You* be grateful to him then because it has nothing to do with me. Parents are *supposed* to provide for their children."

"You self-righteous, little…"

"James! Stop it. Stop this now," her mother cried as she nearly threw the drink at him. "Look at how you're acting.

We finally get Gabby back and you're behaving insufferably."

Gabrielle rose from her chair. "I shouldn't have come."

"No, maybe you shouldn't have," her father responded shortly.

Gabrielle prepared to walk out, but she stopped herself. Despite the vitriol coming from his mouth, she'd come home with a purpose, and she would not be deterred. "Can you give us a minute alone?" she asked her mother.

Her mother looked at her and then at her father. "I don't think that's a good idea."

"It'll be fine. I need to speak to Daddy *alone.*"

"If you're sure…"

Gabrielle nodded and her mother reluctantly left the room.

Gabrielle threw down her purse, folded her arms across her chest and faced her father, who sat resolutely in his chair. "I don't know what your problem is, but I came here to help you."

"Help me?" her father asked.

"Yes, help you," Gabrielle said. "Andrew Jackson stopped by my hotel suite."

"I'm aware."

"So you knew he was coming?" Gabrielle couldn't believe her ears. Her own father had set her up and sent his crook of a boss to blackmail her.

"No, Andrew didn't tell me until after."

"You mean after he asked me to commit corporate espionage to save you from being beaten by the mob?" Gabrielle hissed.

"Yes, after," he answered unapologetically. "So what are you going to do?"

"What do you mean?"

"I mean what *are* you going to do, Gabby?" he asked,

running his fingers through his thick silver afro. "Are you going to help your old man out of a bind, or are you going to feed him to the wolves?"

"It's what you deserve," Gabrielle responded honestly. "But that's not why I'm here."

"Are you here to gloat?" he asked. "At your superiority? That you're at Adams Cosmetics and I've turned into a lowly addict?"

Gabrielle's eyes grew sad. *How had they gotten here?* Her relationship with her parents had been strained at best, but this deterioration was beyond her wildest nightmare. "I can't do this." She reached for her purse that she had thrown unceremoniously across the floor. "I have to go."

Her father rose from his chair and as she passed him, he grabbed her arm. "I need an answer, Gabby. Don't you want to help your old man? Don't you want to be a part of this family again?"

Gabrielle looked down at her arm and then back up at him. She would not be manhandled. "I can't believe you would ask me to do such a horrible thing. Now LET ME GO!"

Her mother came running into the room. "What's going on?"

Her father released her arm and flung her away from him. "Your selfish daughter is what's going on. Why don't you just go, Gabby? We don't need you here. We haven't for a long time."

With tears streaming down her face, Gabrielle rushed out of the house. She didn't realize she was hyperventilating until she was back in the car.

Chapter 5

Gabrielle fretted over the next few days about what to do. What kind of monster was her father? He was offering her his love and a chance to be a family again, the one thing she'd wanted more than anything in the world for the past fifteen years—but only if she betrayed Shane and his family.

She had no one to turn to, no one to confide in about her dilemma. She'd had a few friends in high school, but after Seth's death, people she thought were her friends became distant. She could see the pity in their eyes, pity that she'd lost such a wonderful brother like Seth, who was the star of the football team and well liked by all, while she was the nerd and a social outcast. He'd taken her with him that day only so that she would finally get her nose out of a book and make some friends.

And now, when she desperately needed someone to talk to, she had no one. Even though they'd connected in a short time, she couldn't talk to Courtney. How could she tell Courtney what a hideous thing her father had asked her to do? What would she think of Gabby or her family? And Shane—well that wasn't even a consideration. The only person who came to mind was Mariah, but would she understand? Could she understand how desperately Gabby wanted a family again?

Gabrielle tried to keep her distance at the office because in the back of her mind, no matter how hard she tried to push it down, she was contemplating the unthinkable. Courtney, however, was not to be ignored. She continued to call Gabrielle all week until she finally answered her cell phone.

"Have you changed your mind? Are you thinking of bailing?" Courtney asked. "I left several messages for you this week."

"I know, Courtney, and I'm really sorry. I just have a lot going on personally."

"I understand. And I don't want to push you," Courtney replied. "But do you want to see if there's potential with Shane? A makeover will certainly make him stand up and take notice. Ultimately, it's up to you."

"Francois, I want you to take several inches off," Courtney said to the hairstylist as she ran her fingers through Gabrielle's long hair that fell until just above her butt. Despite all her family drama, Gabrielle had decided to go for the makeover on Saturday because she didn't want to waste another second of her life. If she'd learned anything from losing Seth so young it was that life was short, and she needed to take full advantage of all it had to offer. If Shane Adams turned out to be part of the equation, even better.

They had just finished a four-hour shopping spree at

the finest boutiques that Atlanta had to offer, and Gabrielle now had a wide array of dresses, suits, tops, slacks, lingerie and an innumerable amount of shoes.

"But…" Gabrielle started, but Courtney put a finger to her lips.

"Trust me, I know what I'm doing," she replied. "Then I want you to add several soft brown highlights to bring out the caramel color of her skin tone."

"Absolutely!" Francois said as he walked around the stool Gabrielle was sitting in. "It will suit her well. But you know she needs more than the perfect cut, yes? I mean these eyebrows…" He slid his hands over Gabrielle's bushy eyebrows.

"Of course," Courtney responded, shocked that he would doubt her makeover abilities. "I've arranged a facial, followed by mani-pedis for the both of us and then a makeup application by Viola."

"Sounds like the rest of your day is taken," Francois said. "So let me get to work."

"Oh, yes," Courtney replied. "This is a full-day event."

"Are you going someplace special?" Francois asked, finally acknowledging Gabrielle. She'd thought he'd forgotten she was the actual client sitting in the chair.

"Yes, I'm going to dinner at the Adams family estate."

"Oh…" Francois squealed. "You will absolutely love it. They give the best dinner parties."

"So I've heard."

"Well, let's get you ready for the ball," Francois said, spinning her away from the mirror and pulling out his shears. He hated for his clients to watch him work. All they needed to see was the end result.

Gabrielle's eyes grew large when she saw Francois with the shears. She'd allowed her hair to grow out in Paris because it was easier to deal with. Plus, she'd had the hardest time finding a good hairdresser. And now she was about to part with her long hair. She would be shedding the old Gabrielle and starting anew. Considering what had happened with her parents, she was more than ready for a change. *But what would Shane think? She could only hope he would be dazzled by the new Gabrielle.*

Nearly two hours later, Gabrielle was pleased with the result. Francois definitely had earned his high-priced haircut, because what he'd done to her hair was nothing short of miraculous. He'd turned her once-dull brown hair into a sleek long bob that just touched her shoulders. It was shorter in the front and longer in the back, with light brown highlights. The ponytail he'd cut off would be donated to Locks of Love.

"Well?" Courtney held her breath. "What do you think?"

"I love it!" Gabrielle jumped out of the chair and spun around. "Francois, you are amazing!" She leaned forward and kissed the Frenchman's cheek.

"Thank you," Francois said, touching his chest. "I'm so glad you like it."

A smile spread across Courtney's face. "It really is quite stunning." She knew Francois would do a good job, but this was an entirely new look for Gabby.

"All right, what's next?" Gabrielle was all fired up now.

Courtney grabbed her designer purse that she'd strewn across a chair and said, "Time for our facials and manipedis. Francois, I will see you soon?" She blew him air kisses and headed toward the door, but Gabrielle grabbed her arm.

"We haven't paid Francois."

"Don't worry, I took care of it."

"Courtney." Gabrielle stopped in midwalk. "You've already done so much. I can't let you do this, too." Courtney had paid for her entire new wardrobe, and now this?

"C'mon." Courtney grasped Gabrielle's arm and pulled her to the exit. "I *wanted* to do this for you, so just let me."

"Okay, but I'm paying for the spa," Gabrielle insisted.

Courtney sighed. "Okay, okay. Let's go. We only have a few more hours before the party."

Gabrielle loved the woman staring back at her in the mirror. Between the clothes, hair and now the makeup done by Viola, one of the makeup artists at AC, her look was complete. Gone was the plain Gabrielle she was used to seeing, and in her place was a beautiful, sophisticated woman. The sleek hairdo was accented by soft makeup and finished off with a cobalt-blue jersey strapless dress ruched from the bust down to the bodice. The dress hit right above her knee, while rhinestone sandals adorned her feet. It created a curvaceous silhouette and made her look as if she had curves despite her B-cup-size breasts. She was every bit as sexy as any woman Shane had ever dated. No, better! She was feeling just that good about herself, and it was thanks to one person.

"Courtney." She turned to her new best friend, who was sitting in a pedestal chair at her vanity table while Viola finished her makeup. "How can I ever thank you?"

Courtney turned around to face her. "You don't have to. It was my pleasure."

"Courtney…" Viola huffed as she nearly poked her eye with the eyeliner.

"Sorry." Courtney blushed and turned back around. "Shane will have no idea what, or shall I say *who,* is about to hit him."

Gabrielle walked toward her and sat on a nearby ottoman. "Thank you. But this wasn't just about Shane, it was about me, too. I want to know if my makeover will have a positive effect at the office. And well, Shane? That's just an added benefit."

"It's great to hear you sound so confident," Courtney replied. "I think you'll be the best thing to happen to my brother in a long, long time."

There was a knock on the door.

"Who is it?" Courtney yelled through the door.

"Shane."

Gabrielle's eyes filled with fear. She didn't want Shane to see her now and spoil the reveal, but Courtney calmed her. "Hide in the closet."

Gabrielle quickly rushed into Courtney's walk-in closet. It was filled with clothes and shoes from floor to ceiling.

Shane walked into the bedroom seconds later and regarded his sister. "Hey, you," he said, towering over her on the pedestal. "Where have you been all day?" Usually his sister was right there along with Victor, bossing everyone around for their parties.

"I was working on a special project," Courtney responded.

When Viola was done adding powder to finish her makeup, Courtney spun around. "Why?"

"Well, I don't know," Shane said, pacing the room. "I was just wondering if you'd heard from Gabby. I saw that she was on the guest list, and I could only assume that you'd invited her."

"I did. Is that a problem?"

"Problem?" He shrugged his shoulders dismissively. "Um… I was just hoping to speak with her."

"About?" She waved at Viola, who'd packed up her belongings and headed to the door.

"Must you be so nosy?"

"You're the one who claimed she was your mortal

enemy at perfumery school and who pitched a fit about her joining AC."

Shane shrugged. "That's over now. Gabby and I have found neutral ground." *If you could call sharing an earth-shattering kiss that had rattled him to the core neutral ground, then, yes.* He'd been unable to stop thinking about Gabrielle ever since. "And I was hoping we could build on that. You know, for the sake of the company."

"Oh, yes, for the sake of the company." Courtney smiled knowingly. Her brother must think she was stupid if he didn't think she could tell that his feelings toward Gabby had changed.

"I'll see you downstairs," Shane said on his way out.

Gabrielle emerged with a hopeful smile from the closet. From what she'd heard, Shane was definitely interested in her, and tonight she would push the envelope.

When Shane made it to the great room, the party was already under way. His parents were holding court and Kayla and Ethan had already arrived. Several family friends were already milling about drinking champagne and eating canapés.

Shane glanced around the room but didn't see Gabrielle. He imagined she would have already been there as she was always so prompt. It made him anxious. He was eager to have a conversation with her and finally discuss that night at the lounge. He hadn't wanted his words to be an affront and had merely meant that he didn't think it was a good idea that they get involved. That's what he had intended to tell her, but as he laid eyes on Courtney and Gabby as they walked into the room, Shane realized he might have to eat those words.

What the hell had happened to his sweet Gabby? He

sure didn't know, because this new creature walking toward him was simply stunning.

Gabrielle watched Shane's eyes grow wide as she approached, and it caused butterflies to jump up and down in her stomach. What she saw in his eyes, for the first time, was male appreciation. When she reached him, she smiled. "Shane."

Shane lost all speech. All he could do was merely stare at her. He started at her feet, which were encased in sexy rhinestone sandals, and then slowly he allowed his eyes to wander upward. And what a sight it was. The bright blue dress she wore clung to her slender frame like a glove and revealed a slight peekaboo of pert breasts, which he just so happened to love. There was no mistaking that she was all woman underneath. His eyes ended their journey at her face and her immaculate makeup, from the sparkling shade of pale pink gloss on her lips to her arched eyebrows and blue eye shadow. Her usually long hair had been chopped to her shoulders, but instead of being severe, it hung straight and sleek. He was stunned at the beautiful package standing in front of him.

"Cat got your tongue?" Gabrielle asked when Shane's eyes finally connected with hers after his long perusal.

Now there was the Gabby he remembered, Shane thought. "No," he finally spoke. "I was just taken aback by the sudden change in your appearance. It's really quite remarkable."

"So you expected me to stay an ugly duckling forever?" Gabrielle inquired.

"Of course not, Gabby," Shane replied. "And for your information, you were never an ugly duckling to me."

"Just one you thought you could grope in a dark lounge, but not have openly on your arm?" Gabrielle responded, and the mask of the sophistication she was trying to portray came down for a few moments. She hadn't meant to say exactly how she'd felt that night. It was amazing what self-confidence could do for you.

"Is that how you felt?" Shane was mortified. He'd never, ever thought she would view herself as an ugly secret that he needed to keep quiet. "I'm sorry, because that wasn't how I felt...I mean how I feel."

Gabrielle recovered and smiled. "No worries. There are more than enough prospects here who wouldn't mind spending time in my company, if you'll excuse me." She was taking Courtney's advice and making contact with Shane but leaving him wanting more. She wasn't going to spend the entire night hoping he would fawn all over her—she was supposed to mingle.

She found Courtney, standing next to a Latina woman with jet-black hair, brown eyes and a warm smile. "Gabrielle Burton, I'd like you to meet my BFF, Tea Santiago." Courtney squeezed the other woman's shoulders.

"Happy to meet you," Tea replied, extending her hand, which Gabrielle shook.

"So, how did it go?" Courtney asked.

"How did what go?" Tea looked back and forth to both women for an explanation.

"My sister is trying to win Shane's attention," Courtney replied, smiling.

Tea laughed heartily. "Well, that's no easy feat." In the ten years she'd known Courtney, she'd seen dozens of women try, and fail, to win Shane's affection.

"Shane was intrigued," Gabrielle answered.

Courtney glanced over Tea's shoulder. "He seems so. That's good. Now here's what you have to do to keep him wanting more." She whispered in Gabrielle's ear.

* * *

Shane watched from the other side of the room as Gabby, Courtney and Tea appeared to be in a deep conversation. He should have known Courtney had something to do with Gabby's transformation. His little sister just couldn't stay out of folks' business. He was going to have to have a word with her.

"Did you see Gabrielle Burton?" Kayla asked as she suddenly joined him. "She looks sensational!"

"Yeah." Shane turned away to face another direction.

Kayla asked, "What is wrong with Gabrielle getting a makeover? If you ask me, she needed a little fine-tuning."

"That's the problem," Shane replied, sipping his drink. "Before, I could rationalize not getting involved with her, but now…"

"But now, what?" Kayla stared in Shane's eyes.

"But with her—" he pointed to Gabby with his drink "—looking like that…that sexy, I don't know, Kay. It's going to be difficult to keep my promise to stay away from her."

Kayla understood and nodded in agreement. "Looks like you have a problem, Watson."

"Ya think?"

Shane did his best to keep his distance during the course of the cocktail hour, and when it came time for dinner, he intended to sit farther down the long table in the formal dining room, next to his mother. But Courtney beat him to the punch, which meant he was going to have to sit opposite Gabby.

Gabrielle smiled at him once and then continued talking to her dinner companion, who just so happened to be Ethan's right-hand man, Daniel Walker. Daniel was a fine-looking man any woman wouldn't mind spending time with, which irked Shane even more. Gabby appeared to be enjoying his every word. She was so engrossed in their conversation, she didn't even hear Shane ask her to pass the vinaigrette.

"Oh, I'm sorry." Gabrielle batted her eyelashes at Shane. "Here you go." She leaned across the table to hand him the boat, and when she did their hands touched for the merest of seconds. A jolt of electricity shot right through her, and she snatched her hand back. She glanced up and found Shane watching her intently, which meant he must have felt it, too. The sexual tension between them was palpable, so much so that by the time dessert was served Gabrielle had to excuse herself. Although she appreciated the attention Daniel was bestowing on her thanks to her makeover, she couldn't take the look of raw hunger scorched in Shane's eyes every time she glanced in his direction.

In the powder room, she began counting from one to one hundred to calm her frayed nerves. Sure, she'd transformed herself so that Shane would be interested in her, but now that he was, she was afraid to go down that road. But she could and would seduce him. She was a worldly woman, well capable of handling Shane Adams.

When Gabrielle finally exited, she made her way back toward the dining room, but a lone figure stood in the hall waiting for her. From the silhouette, she could tell it was a male form. It was Shane.

Gabrielle swallowed hard, but didn't back down and walked toward him. "Shane, what are you doing out here? You're missing dessert."

Shane stared back at Gabrielle in the snug-fitting dress with rhinestones dripping from her ears and wanted to back her up against one of the walls, pull that dress up and have his way with her right then and there. But he instead said, "Why don't we go for a walk on the grounds?"

"A walk?" Gabrielle asked. "Sounds good, but…"

Shane didn't wait for her answer, because he'd already intertwined his fingers with hers and was leading her down the hall.

"What will everyone think?" Gabrielle asked, glancing behind her.

"That we needed time alone," Shane responded huskily as he led her out onto the terrace and into the gardens.

Gabrielle didn't know what to make of their holding hands. It was an innocent enough gesture, yet there was something intimate about it, especially when he gave her hand a little squeeze and gently stroked the sensitive skin in the inside of her wrist as they walked.

"The garden is my mother's domain," Shane said when they came to a small private garden. "She loves her roses."

"They're beautiful," Gabrielle said as she fingered one of the petals. He released her hand only when she stopped to smell the different kinds of roses. When she finally stood back up, she found Shane had come closer to her.

"Why did you come here tonight?" Shane asked.

"Courtney invited me."

Shane shook his head. "That's not the only reason you're here."

"What other reason would there be?"

"Well, maybe you came here for me?" Shane stared at her. He watched the rapid rise and fall of her breasts in the strapless dress and knew he was right. Gabrielle had come here tonight to seduce him with her new look, and she'd succeeded. He desired her. *But would she back out of what she'd started?*

"Is there no end to your arrogance?" Gabrielle asked, a little too unsteadily for her liking, given the way Shane was looking at her as if she was dessert.

"No, which is why I know you're going to enjoy this,"

Shane said. He circled his arm around her waist seconds before his lips descended on hers. The hunger behind his kiss caused her to respond, and when his lips moved more firmly over hers, seeking entry into her mouth, she parted them, giving him complete access to anything and everything he wanted. Shane was slow at first, grazing and tasting before touching his tongue with hers, but when he did, it was like a missile shot right through to her core.

Her dreams of being thoroughly kissed by Shane couldn't compare with the reality. He was relentless with his kiss, touching every crevice of her mouth and sucking on her bottom lip. Gabrielle's breasts grew hot and heavy at his searing kiss, and she felt her nipples turn into hardened peaks underneath her dress. Dampness began gathering down below and she began to tremble.

But just when she was really getting into the kiss, Shane suddenly pulled away. If he didn't stop, he'd be tossing his jacket on the ground, pulling Gabby down onto it and making love to her until she screamed out his name.

"Why did you stop?" Gabrielle was disappointed. Was he pulling away again? *Did he not want her?* She'd thought the desire between them was obvious. Mutual.

"Not here," Shane said, clenching his fists at his side and then releasing them. "Come with me." He grasped her hand again.

"Where?" Gabrielle asked breathlessly, taking his hand. She wanted to be with Shane and didn't want to waste another moment.

"Follow me." Although his body was shaking with desire, somehow he managed to lead her down a winding walkway.

Gabrielle had to nearly trot to keep up with him in her stiletto sandals before arriving at the Olympic-size family pool. "The pool?" She smiled. "Um… That's really out in the open."

"No, silly." Shane smiled at her naïveté. "The pool house." He nodded in the direction of the small house next to the pool. He walked over, pulled out a key and inserted it into the lock.

Before Gabrielle could hesitate, he swiftly spun her into the room, closing the door behind them. Shane gently pushed her backward against the door, meshing their bodies together. Despite their clothes, Gabrielle could feel Shane's burgeoning erection in his pants. She was surprised, yet proud, that she could turn him on in that way.

"I want you so much," Shane murmured in her ear as he slid one hand behind her head to bring her closer to his face. He bent his head and leaned down to give her a deliciously sinful kiss filled with passion and the promise of more to come.

Gabrielle didn't respond with words; she responded with action. She slid her tongue inside his warm, waiting mouth and fused her tongue with his. Shane moaned aloud and Gabrielle shuddered in response. "I want you, too," she murmured.

He reached behind her and grabbed her buttocks to bring her body in direct contact with his erection. Slowly, he began to grind against her, causing delicious friction between their bodies. With each deliberate thrust of his groin against her, she swayed and desire built. Gabrielle savored each delicious sensation and whimpered.

When Shane lifted her dress to her waist so he could stroke her thighs, Gabrielle didn't stop him. She'd always wondered what it was about Shane that had women aflutter, and she was about to find out if he lived up to the hype.

Shane started with one of Gabby's legs, stroking the side before moving up to her thighs. Her skin felt soft and silky to Shane's touch and he wanted more. He continued his quest until he reached his destination and when he did, he wasted no time pushing the tiny fabric that was her thong aside and dipping his finger inside her. Gabby was already moist, and he intended to make her even wetter.

He slid one finger inside her slowly at first in a come-hither motion until she began to move against him. When Gabby began moaning aloud, Shane knew he'd reached her sweet spot, and he stroked her harder and faster until she clutched at the lapels on his tuxedo jacket, eager for release. And with several quick successive strokes, he gave it to her, and she cried out his name.

"Shane!"

"Yes, baby." Shane bent down to her neck. He breathed in the floral scent of her perfume before pressing his lips against her slender neck and sucking it. Shane moved from Gabby's neck to her ear, lightly stroking it with quick flicks of his hot tongue.

"Oh…" Gabrielle moaned, clutching Shane's jacket with one hand and the back of his head with the other. When he returned his lips to hers and traced them with his tongue, she took the hint and immediately parted her lips to allow him entry. And once inside, she stroked her tongue with his and they kissed like two randy teenagers. But Shane quickly turned the tables, taking her tongue in his mouth and sucking on it as if he was a newborn babe. It felt delicious and wicked, and Gabrielle mimicked him by doing the same.

Gabrielle barely had time to come back down to earth from her first orgasm when Shane began pushing her toward the bed. The pool house was small, but it had an open floor plan that included a bedroom area with a king-size bed, a small living room and a kitchen with a break-fast nook. Before she knew it, they were both flying down onto the bed in a heap of arms and legs. She feverishly pushed off Shane's jacket, reaching for the buttons on his tuxedo shirt and sliding the shirt over his muscular shoulders. It ended up on the floor, as the rest of their clothes were about to.

Shane eased the zipper of her dress down her back, pushing it down to her waist and feasting his eyes on her bare breasts, beautiful twins that he intended to lap up with his tongue and tease with his teeth. She helped him by lifting her hips so he could slide the dress over her slender hips and down to her feet. He tossed it aside and quickly hooked his fingers on her thong and tugged it down her legs.

When she was as naked as the day she was born, Shane was happy. And he was hungry for her. He'd had lascivious thoughts about what he wanted to do her body all during dinner, and he intended to live every one of them out.

"Are you sure about this?" Shane asked, looking down at Gabby on the bed. "Because there's still time…" He looked down at his erection that was poking through his pants. "Barely…if you want to change your mind."

Gabrielle shook her head. "I don't want to change my mind. I want this. I want you." She scooted to the edge of the bed and reached for his pants. She unbuttoned his pants and pulled them down his legs so he could step out of them. His briefs were next, and it gave Gabrielle a chance to caress the curves of Shane's firm buttocks.

Shane smiled broadly. "Good. 'Cause I need you bad." In the briefest of seconds, he'd lowered his full weight back onto the bed.

Gabrielle grabbed the back of his head and brought his mouth back down on hers. She slid her tongue inside his mouth and stroked hers with his while Shane was sliding his hand down her side to her hip.

"Are you ready to come for me again?" Shane whispered in her ear when he reached the damp folds at the center of her. He stroked them with light circles and watched her eyes dilate and her hips writhe restlessly.

"No fair," Gabrielle said, trying to clamp her legs shut. "I haven't been able to return the favor."

"You will in time." Shane left her lips and bent down to push her legs open again and brush his fingers across the dark curls. She made whimpering noises as if she wanted him to quit, but he didn't. He slipped one finger deeper and deeper inside her until she clenched around him. That's when Shane placed his mouth where his fingers had been and began to flick his tongue across her tight nub. Gabby nearly jumped.

"Ohmigod!"

"Easy, baby." Shane grasped her hips and began tonguing her further.

The pressure of Shane's tongue increased and matched his fingers, and Gabrielle could no longer hold in her release. She screamed out his name again and again. "Shane! Shane!"

"Yes, baby?" he asked, looking up at her.

"Now!" Gabrielle murmured.

"I hear you." Shane knew exactly what Gabrielle meant, because he was thick and erect and needed a release, but he had wanted to make sure she was pleased first. He leaned down and reached into his tuxedo jacket pocket for a condom, sheathed himself and returned to the bed.

Gabrielle was looking up at him with those adorable brown eyes of hers and Shane was lost. With his weight on his forearms, he leaned down to kiss her just as he entered her in one smooth thrust. She was moist and ready for him, easily accepting all of him. She felt so good that

Shane immediately began moving deep inside her. *Had anyone ever felt this good, this tight, this right?*

Gabrielle picked up his rhythm, wrapped her legs around his and matched each thrust by lifting her hips. Each thrust brought Shane higher and higher, and all thought and reason about whether this was right or wrong flew out the window. All he could think about was being in this moment with Gabby. She gyrated her hips against him and he thrust harder and faster, until his world exploded around him.

Sometime during the course of the night, Gabrielle awoke to find Shane's hard-as-a-rock erection beside her and ready for action again. This time, Gabrielle took control, and before Shane could object, she took him inside her mouth. She wanted all of Shane and continued to tease his penis by pulling in and out slowly.

"Gabby," Shane moaned, grabbing a handful of Gabrielle's hair in his hand. "Oh, yes, baby, just like that."

Gabrielle moved her lips up and down his hardened manhood, until Shane pulled her away. He grabbed another condom and slid it over his incredibly sensitive member and lay back on the bed.

"Straddle me," he commanded, pulling her over him.

Gabrielle looked down at Shane; his face was dark with desire. "With pleasure," she said and slid herself down on him, allowing him to fill her completely.

"That's right, ride me, baby." Shane wrapped his arms around her waist and helped her move.

Gabrielle closed her eyes and lived in the moment, rocking her hips and riding him back and forth. Delicious sensations ripped through her and her trembling limbs clung to him. Shane's demanding lips touched hers, and it was like the flame that melted hot wax. Her lips burned in the aftermath of his possession. And when Shane circled his hands around her waist and tugged at her breasts with his mouth, Gabrielle moaned her pleasure and ran her fingers through his short curly fro. Shane took the hint and teased the peaks with light flicks of his tongue, causing tension to grow deeper and deeper inside Gabrielle.

Shane continued pumping his hips to meet Gabrielle's motions, and it didn't take long for her to splinter in his arms. The most intense pleasure she'd ever experienced in her life washed over her, and Gabrielle cried out and fell across Shane's chest.

She'd never had such a spectacular climax before. Making love with Shane was the most incredible sex of her life, and she was beyond satiated. The last thing Gabrielle remembered was Shane brushing his lips across hers before she drifted off to sleep.

Chapter 6

When Gabrielle awoke the next morning and wiped the sleep from her eyes, she didn't remember where she was, but then she felt the ache between her thighs and all the memories of her hot night of passion with Shane came flooding back.

She wanted to stay in bed forever and relive the memories. Relive Shane's touch, his kiss, his every caress, but she couldn't because when she reached over for him, he was gone.

Slowly, she rose from the bed, pulling the sheet around her bosom. She glanced at her reflection in the nearby mirror. She looked a sight, much different from the beautiful creature Courtney had created the night before. *What would Shane think now in the morning light? Would he regret making love to her?*

Gabrielle didn't want to find out. She quickly picked up her lacy thong and her cobalt-blue dress off the ceramic tile and dressed. She was about to make a quick getaway, but Shane came barreling through the pool-house door, bare chested and wearing only his tuxedo pants from the night before. He was holding two cups of what she could only imagine was coffee.

"Good morning, beautiful," Shane said, coming forward to plant a kiss across her stunned lips. "Sorry I had to leave, but there wasn't much in the way of accommodations here." He held out a mug for her to take.

Why did he have to look so handsome in the morning light, while she looked like a wanton woman with her swollen lips and tousled hair?

"Good morning," she mumbled, accepting the mug, dropping her clothes to the floor.

"So where do you think you're going?" he asked, walking over to the breakfast bar and having a seat on the stool.

"Home."

Shane's brow furrowed. "Why?" He sipped on his steaming hot cup of coffee and then glanced back up at her.

"Well, last night was fun…" Gabrielle began, "but…"

"It doesn't have to end," Shane finished. "I thoroughly enjoyed last night."

"You did?"

"Don't sound so shocked," Shane said. "Last night was pretty incredible. I wasn't the only one who had multiple orgasms, was I?" In fact, Shane had quite enjoyed watching Gabby get off. She was so expressive when they'd made love that he'd been completely turned on just by watching her.

Gabrielle's cheeks became flush with crimson. She wasn't a prude, but yet she wasn't used to a man talking so openly about sex. "No, you weren't."

"Well, then, since we both enjoyed ourselves, I see no reason why we can't do this again."

"I can," Gabrielle replied. "How about the fact that we

work together? You are my boss." As much as she wanted Shane, the situation could get complicated very quickly if one of them got their feelings hurt. And, more than likely, that would be her.

"True, but if it's mutual, I don't see a problem."

"I need to think about this," Gabrielle replied, placing the mug on the granite countertop. As much as she wanted this, last night had completely exceeded her expectations, and she needed to evaluate the situation. She went to walk past Shane to the bathroom, but he circled his arm around her waist.

"Why don't I remind you of last night and give you something to think about?" Shane lifted Gabby off her feet so suddenly, her clothes and shoes fell to the floor with a thud before he placed her back on the massive king-size bed.

"Shane..." Gabrielle began, but before she could utter another word, Shane was smothering her lips with a searing kiss that made her toes curl. But it was when he reached out and gently stroked her face and said, "You're beautiful, Gabby. You always have been" that Gabrielle thought she might cry. But that never happened, because the storm that was Shane came toward her and pulled the sheet away to reveal her naked bosom before sliding his tuxedo pants down to his waiting erection. The rest was a blur of two hot, sweaty bodies joined together as one, riding wave after wave of ecstasy. Each wave causing screams of passion to be wrenched from Gabrielle's throat as she held on to Shane's rock-hard butt as he dove deeper and deeper inside her.

When it was over, they were bathed in sweat and Gabby was spent. Eventually, Gabrielle headed for the shower, but Shane didn't give her any peace.

"Did you think you were going to shower alone?" he

asked, pulling back the curtain. He shook his head. "I don't think so." He hoisted her atop his waist, backed her up against the wall and had his way with her.

Later that evening, Shane sat down to dinner with the family at Kayla and Ethan's estate in Tuxedo Park. Their father had finally agreed to a dinner invitation, mostly because their mother wanted to see the progress that Kayla had made on the nursery and refused to let the animosity that Byron still carried for Ethan prevent her from missing out on her duties as a grandmother.

"Someone sure looks like the cat who ate the canary," Courtney commented from across the table as Kayla passed the platter of duck breast with plum demi-glace that her chef had prepared. She had earlier tried unsuccessfully to get the scoop from the lady herself, but Gabrielle was being surprisingly quiet.

"What *are* you talking about, Courtney?" Shane inquired, taking the platter. He helped himself to a piece before passing it to Ethan.

"You!" She pointed to him. "Look at you. If it were possible for a man to glow, you would be. Did you get yourself some last night?"

"Courtney!" Their mother's voice rang out from across the table. "That is not appropriate dinner conversation."

Courtney shrugged. "I was just wondering where Shane escaped to after dinner last night is all."

"Hmm… You *were* conspicuously absent after dinner," Kayla teased. She noticed he'd disappeared after dessert, but then again, so had Gabrielle Burton. *Had something happened between them?* Kayla stared directly at Shane, but he refused to look at her and turned his eyes elsewhere.

"That's my business, little sis," Shane commented,

reaching for the bottle of cabernet and pouring himself a generous glass.

Courtney threw up her hands. "All right, you're no fun. I'll leave you to your secrets."

"Much obliged."

"Who I want to talk about is that lovely creature Gabrielle Burton," Byron Adams said from the head of the table. He'd been surprised when Ethan had offered up his seat earlier, deferring to him as the head of the family. He'd accepted the seat with a handshake. He was trying for the sake of his daughter and soon-to-be grandchild to forget how Ethan Graham had come to be a part of the family and remember that Ethan had once been like a surrogate son to him. "From what you'd told us about her, Shane, I'd thought she wasn't going to be very attractive, but she was absolutely stunning, if you ask me." Then Byron turned to his wife, "But of course, not as beautiful as you, my dear."

A broad smile spread across Elizabeth's face. "Of course not."

"Really?" Shane asked. "I hadn't noticed."

Courtney coughed loudly and reached for her water glass. Her brother was a bold-faced liar and she knew it, but she wasn't going to call him out in front of the family. Shane had been anything but unaffected by Gabby's makeover.

"I, for one, sure did," Ethan responded from the other side of the table, and all eyes turned to him. "It's like a lightbulb went off in her head and she realized what a little makeup, a good haircut and the right dress can do. If you had seen her before, Byron, it's a night-and-day difference."

"Sometimes we women need to switch our style up," Elizabeth offered, in an attempt to defend Gabby. "You know, keep you men interested and on your toes."

"Mom…" Kayla blushed.

"C'mon, my dear," her mother replied. "How else do you think your father and I keep the home fires burning after thirty-six years of marriage?"

Shane put his hands over his ears. "We don't want to know, Mama."

"All I can say is there are going to be a number of men at the office who will be standing up and taking notice," Ethan said.

"And would one of them be you?" Kayla raised an eyebrow.

"Oh, no, baby." Ethan reached across the table and squeezed her hand. "I only have eyes for you and my son in there."

"I don't think that would be wise for any of them," Shane replied. He didn't want any other man looking at Gabrielle, much less talking to her. But he couldn't say that, so he said instead, "A workplace romance is ill-advised."

"Is that so?" Courtney smirked from his side.

Shane rolled his eyes. Courtney clearly knew what had transpired between him and Gabrielle. He could see she was itching to say something, but was thankful she was showing restraint, which wasn't her usual M.O.

"Actually, I'm glad you're all here," Ethan said. "I heard some disconcerting news that you might be interested to know."

"What's going on, babe?" Kayla inquired.

"I've heard rumors that Jax Cosmetics is launching their own fragrance."

"Really?" Shane asked. *And why was this the first time he was hearing about this?*

"Of course." Byron wiped his mouth and threw down

his napkin. "That man wouldn't know innovation if it slapped him in the face."

"A fragrance line for a cosmetics company is not unheard of," Ethan responded.

Byron ignored Ethan's comment and jumped out of his seat. "You know why he's doing this, don't you?" He turned to his wife. "Andrew could never accept that I stole you away from him, and now instead of coming at me directly, he's trying to copy us."

"Well, you know the saying that imitation is the sincerest form of flattery," Courtney interjected, attempting to lighten the mood. She knew of the animosity between her father and Andrew Jackson.

"Dad, don't worry," Shane replied calmly. "Andrew doesn't have half the talent in his lab that we have at Adams Cosmetics."

"Exactly!" Kayla pointed to her brother. "Jax Cosmetics has always come in second, hell, even third by consumers. They don't stand a chance against Hypnotic or the new fragrance that Shane is developing."

"I trust in the quality of your work, Shane," Byron said, pacing the floor. "But I don't trust that man! And the timing of this is suspect. He must be looking for a chink in our armor."

"He won't find it," Shane said firmly. "I have a solid team of chemists behind me." When they'd combined Graham International cosmetic division with Adam Cosmetics, his staff had doubled.

"And you're sure they're happy?" Ethan asked. "Because I wouldn't put it past Andrew to try to steal one of them."

Kayla shook her head. "Trust me, that's not even possible. You know that Adams Cosmetics is a family company. It's what you—" she pointed to her father "—what all of us—" she pointed to the family surrounding the table "—promote. He will not find a chink in our armor. But perhaps you should meet with everyone individually, Shane. You know, make sure they're happy."

"I trust my team," Shane said testily. He couldn't imagine any one of them going to work for Jax Cosmetics. Shane glanced around the room and noted several concerned looks. "But if it will appease you all, I will speak with them."

"Good." Byron sat back down to the table. His wife reached across the table and squeezed his hand and he smiled back. He was a very lucky man, and that's why he knew they had to watch their backs. Andrew Jackson was not above pulling a fast one.

Gabrielle was on a natural high. Last night with Shane had been everything she'd anticipated and then some. They'd come together with a fiery passion at first and then he'd softened his lovemaking. Kissing, touching and tasting, nibbling every single part of her. Her skin still burned from where he'd touched her, and if she closed her eyes she could still feel his lips on hers. He'd completely put his stamp on her, and she was walking around in a daze.

Somehow she'd made it back to her hotel room to take another shower. Now she was lying on the bed with the Sunday paper, looking over the classifieds for apartments. Of course, Courtney had volunteered to have a friend she knew in real estate help her, but Gabrielle figured she'd look in the paper, as well. She was perusing the classifieds when her cell phone rang.

"Hey, stranger," Mariah replied from the other end.

"Mariah." A smile spread across Gabrielle's face at hearing her friend's voice. "It's so good to hear from you."

"Wish I could say the same thing. I haven't heard from you in weeks," Mariah chastised.

"I'm so sorry," Gabrielle said, sitting up in her bed. "It's been a little crazy around here."

"Oh, yeah, how's the new job going?"

"Wonderfully, if you can believe that."

"Really?" Mariah was surprised, given the rivalry Gabrielle and Shane once shared. "I thought you and Shane were like oil and water."

"Not anymore."

There was silence for several seconds before Mariah said, "Did you hook up with Shane?"

Gabrielle was dying to talk to someone other than Courtney about Shane and couldn't resist confessing. "Yes, and I have to tell you, it was well worth the wait!"

"Get out of here! When did this happen?"

"Last night, if you can believe that," Gabrielle replied. "We spent the entire night and all of this morning in bed. This man was so incredible with his hands and tongue and…"

"Wow!" Mariah exclaimed. "It's getting a little hot. You've got me fanning myself over here."

"You're telling me." Gabrielle laughed and fell back onto the pillows. "It was pretty amazing, and I have his sister to thank for getting him to notice me."

"How so?"

"I agreed to a makeover."

"You?" Mariah said. "No way. I've always wanted to give you a makeover, but you've always been so adamant about being natural and true to yourself. What changed?"

"Everything changed when Shane kissed me one night after work, but then apologized for it. It made me think I wasn't good enough for him, so I decided to change a few things. I cut my hair."

"Not your beautiful curls?"

"Oh, yes," Gabrielle responded. "I donated them to Locks of Love, put on some makeup and bought an entirely new wardrobe. That's when Shane had no choice but to notice me. He even got jealous when he saw me with another man."

"I'm so glad you finally let loose, girlfriend. That was long overdue. Are you guys going to continue seeing each other?"

Gabrielle shrugged. "Haven't decided yet."

"I say go for it!" Mariah said. "With a man that fine, you can't go wrong."

Gabrielle chuckled. Trust Mariah to keep it real and say exactly how she felt. "I know. I just have to think it through."

"Don't take too long," Mariah replied. "Otherwise someone else might come in there and snatch him up."

After Gabrielle hung up, she realized Mariah was right. Shane Adams was one of Atlanta's most eligible bachelors and wouldn't be single for long. She was going to have to decide. And soon.

Gabrielle didn't run into Shane until late Monday morning. She'd sat in bed the night before, wondering how they would act working together in such a confined space for long periods. But she shouldn't have worried, because Shane came in all businesslike, as if they hadn't spent the better part of Sunday morning wrapped up in each other's arms.

"Good morning, Gabrielle," Shane said as he nodded at her when he entered the room.

"Morning." Gabrielle didn't look up from the test tubes she was testing. She couldn't, because if she did, she thought everyone in the lab would be able to see her blush and know that they had been intimate.

Several coworkers had complimented her on her new look, and she noticed a few of the male chemists who had never paid an ounce of attention admiring her new form-flattering wrap dress that showed a long expanse of leg.

Shane noticed Gabrielle as soon as he walked in. He was trying hard to be impartial, but it was difficult. She was wearing a body-hugging dress and the material clung to her tight behind. A behind he remembered all too well.

Gabrielle had barely hazarded a glance up at him when he spoke. *Was she regretting the night they'd shared?* Although he hadn't meant for it to happen, he hadn't regretted it. And the more he thought about it, if they were discreet, he didn't see any reason for them not to continue seeing each other, as long as Gabby understood that the relationship would last for a few months and no more. He didn't do commitment longer than that. For some reason, he didn't seem to be wired that way.

He saw his parents' marriage and knew it was possible, but the kind of love they shared was one in a million. He doubted there was a woman alive who could keep him intrigued for a lifetime.

Shane shook his head to clear his mind, because he needed to focus. He needed to speak with all the chemists in the lab and ensure everyone was satisfied. Content. And ensure that Andrew Jackson would not find a defector in the bunch.

And that's exactly what he did for the remainder of the day. At first, his staff had thought they'd done something wrong when they were called into his office one by one. But eventually they all relaxed and assured Shane that they loved their job at AC, because their input was valued and the benefits were exceptional.

Shane made sure that Gabrielle was his last interview near the end of the day. She'd worked professionally, yet quietly, throughout the course of the day. A few times, he'd caught her staring at him and he was sure she was remembering exactly what he did, the sweet sensation of their bodies joined as one. He wondered if she was eager to repeat it or if she'd decided that one night with him was enough.

One night wasn't enough for Shane. He wanted Gabby back in his bed. He wanted to see her look at him again as if he was the only man in the world for her. He wanted to feel her cuddled next to him in the crook of his arm. He wanted to hear the whimpering noises she made when his fingers were inside her and she came and see the arousal cross her face as he thrust inside her.

"You wanted to see me?" Gabrielle asked. It was the end of the day and Gabrielle had been on pins and needles. Everyone else had been called into Shane's office except her. The blinds to his windows had been shut for absolute privacy all day. Was this a bad omen?

"Come in." Shane waved her inside his office, which was located behind the laboratory. "Close the door."

Gabrielle inhaled sharply before closing the door behind her. "Is there a problem?" she asked, standing nervously at the door. She shifted back and forth uncomfortably on her heels.

"The only problem is this." Shane swiftly jumped up from his seat, closed the distance between them and dipped his head so his lips could find hers.

Gabrielle pulled away. "Shane… We're in the office." She glanced at the door. "What if someone walked in and saw us?"

Shane sighed. She was right of course, but he hadn't been able to help himself. The way she'd been nervously

standing there had been the Gabby of old and not the se-
ductress he'd seen at the Adams estate. He wasn't sure
which he preferred. Maybe it was both, because then he
didn't know what to expect. "I'm sorry. It's just that I've
been wanting to do that all day."

Gabrielle smiled. Well, at least she knew Shane was still
thinking of her and the composed facade he'd presented
all day had been for show.

"Have you given any more thought to my proposal?"
Shane asked.

"Is that why you called me in here?"

Shane sighed. Gabby obviously wasn't ready to tell him
her decision. "Actually, it wasn't." Reluctantly, he returned
to his desk and plopped down in his chair. He would have
to abide by the book at work. "Please have a seat." He motioned for her to sit in the chair opposite his desk.

"Is something wrong? Are you unhappy with my per-
formance?" Gabrielle inquired. "I mean, you've called everyone into your office today."

Shane shook his head. "Quite the opposite. You're all
doing phenomenal work. I just want to make sure everyone
is happy, and if they're not I want to rectify it. We have a
great team here and I wouldn't want to lose anyone."

Gabrielle listened to what Shane wasn't saying and immediately understood. "Are you concerned that someone
might leave and go to a competitor?"

"Why would you think that?"

"C'mon, Shane. I worked for L'Oréal. Chemists were
stolen all the time by competitors."

Shane nodded. "That doesn't happen here at AC. We
run a tight ship. Everyone in that room—" Shane pointed
to the door "—has been a part of the AC family for five
years or more. We believe in rewarding talent and com-
pensating accordingly."

Gabrielle smiled. "I know, which is why I came here. But even you must realize that nothing is ever guaranteed."

Shane frowned. "Have you been approached?"

Immediately, Gabrielle's stomach sunk. Yes, she had, but she could never tell Shane that, or why for that matter. He would never understand the debt of gratitude her family owed to Jax Cosmetics. "No," she answered instead. "And if I were, I'm happy here."

"Even being second in command?" Shane pressed.

Gabrielle thought back to his comment on day one. "Yes, even if I'm second in command."

Shane released a cautious sigh. "Glad to hear it. I think you're a talented chemist, Gabby."

"You do?"

"Yes, I mean it. This has nothing to do with our personal relationship, wherever that may lead." He stared into her eyes, desperate for her to believe him. He respected her a great deal and she needed to know that.

"Thank you." Gabrielle smiled back. "Well, I have to go."

"How about dinner?" Shane asked.

"I have plans," Gabrielle replied. "Maybe one day next week." And with that comment, Gabrielle reluctantly headed for the door. Once she was out of Shane's office, Gabrielle wanted to kick herself. She would love nothing more than to have dinner with Shane, but she remembered Courtney's advice about her brother liking a challenge. She wasn't going to make it easy for him, especially since she wasn't even sure where she wanted things to go.

Chapter 7

As Gabrielle waited for Andrew Jackson at a small diner in Marietta on Saturday morning, she knew how she needed to handle her father's request. She'd chosen the location because she couldn't afford for anyone to see the two of them together. Although she had nothing to be ashamed of, she didn't want anyone to misinterpret the meeting.

She'd agonized over it, but knew she'd made the right decision. She couldn't and she wouldn't betray Shane or the Adams family, not after everything they'd done for her. Ethan and Kayla had brought her back to the States and given her a great opportunity at Adams Cosmetics. Courtney had single-handedly transformed her life, and now she was embarking on a possible relationship with Shane Adams, the one man she'd always secretly dreamed of. She couldn't risk it, not even for her family.

Andrew Jackson walked into the small diner, and his towering presence filled the small space. He was wearing blue jeans, a red cotton shirt, black leather jacket and cowboy boots. "I'll have coffee, black," he yelled to the waitress behind the counter, before sliding into the booth opposite Gabrielle.

"Gabrielle," Andrew said. "I hope you have good news for me." He gave her a plastic smile that she could see straight through.

The waitress came over with a coffee cup and poured Andrew a cup out of her carafe. "Would you care for anything else?"

Andrew glanced at Gabrielle, but she shook her head. "That'll be all." The waitress nodded and walked back to the counter.

"So, what's it going to be?" He took a generous swallow of his black coffee.

"You're going to have to find yourself another lackey," Gabrielle responded evenly.

"You're refusing to help your father?" Andrew replied. "You really are one coldhearted…"

Gabrielle held up her hand. "No need to resort to name-calling, Mr. Jackson. It's rather uncouth, don't you think?" She narrowed her eyes. "You put my father, heck my entire family, up to doing your dirty work. If you want to come after the Adams family, why don't you have the courage to do so by creating products that will compete with them, instead of trying to steal theirs?"

Andrew laughed and slid his fingers through his slick black hair, but his dark eyes never left hers. "You know, I like you, Ms. Burton. You have a lot of spunk and I'd love to have you on my team, but since you're determined to stay with the Adams lot, I have no choice but to ruin you, too."

"Excuse me?" Gabrielle said. She saw a shadow outside

the window and turned around long enough for a photographer to snap a photograph of her and Andrew together.

"Did you think I didn't realize why you wanted to meet me out here in the boondocks?" Andrew asked. "You didn't want anyone to know we'd met, and now I have evidence that we did. Might be beneficial to me in the future, don'tcha think? In the meantime, don't you worry your pretty little head about the products at Jax Cosmetics, 'cause I always have a backup plan." He rose from the booth, guzzled the last drop of coffee in the cup and returned it to the table. "You have a fine day now."

Gabrielle leaned back in the booth. *Andrew Jackson was a dangerous man, and she'd just made a powerful enemy.*

Shane watched Gabrielle from inside his office. It had taken a month since her hire, but they'd finally settled on Ecstasy, the new fragrance to be launched after Hypnotic's huge debut. He was overjoyed that he could finally tell Ethan and Kayla, who were insisting since Gabby came aboard, that they had a winner.

Despite his excitement, he was still antsy. Could it be because it had been nearly two weeks since he and Gabrielle had spent the night together? Shane didn't know what had happened, but after their talk in his office, Gabby had been distant. It was as if she hadn't wanted to be near him, much less in the same room with him. *What could have happened to cool her desire for him?*

He knew Gabrielle was not immune to him. Perhaps it was time he let her know exactly what she was missing. Once the last chemist had left the lab and Gabrielle remained, finishing a test, Shane made his move.

He left his office and came into the laboratory. "How are the tests coming along for the new lotion?"

"Um…fine," Gabrielle said, not looking up from her microscope.

"That's good," Shane said, walking toward the exit. He locked the laboratory door and turned to stare at Gabby, who was bent over the counter. He loved the curve of her backside even when she was wearing a lab coat, but in his opinion she was wearing too many clothes. He intended to rectify that.

He strolled toward her until he was inches away from her. It was then that Gabrielle finally looked up.

"Shane?" She took several steps backward and tried to lunge away, but Shane pressed her against the counter and lowered his head.

Gabrielle expected a powerful kiss, but Shane took his time. Slowly, he sipped at her lower lip, and then the top lip with his tongue until she released a sigh of pure delight, allowing him easy entrance to her mouth. Gabrielle welcomed the invasion and didn't realize just how much she needed this until Shane's tongue was merging with hers. His tongue rubbed over hers again and again, and she found herself helpless but to give in and move against him. Snaking her arms around his neck, she nestled closer to his broad chest.

Shane's hands began a slow descent until they came to rest on her backside. He molded the mounds with his hands, Gabrielle trembled and he could feel her entire body spark to life. He pulled her silk shirt from her skirt and fondled her breasts underneath until he felt them become hard and pucker to tight pebbles. They were pert and ready for attention. His attention. Shane unbuttoned her shirt and placed his mouth over one tight pucker through her bra and tugged gently.

"Oh…" Gabrielle moaned.

Shane pushed aside the wisp of satin fabric and his

mouth closed around her nipple. He pulled the nipple deeper and deeper into his mouth and pressed her flesh against him so she could feel the firm ridge of his manhood, and Gabrielle nearly exploded. She'd seriously missed being with him.

Quickly, Gabrielle began fumbling with the buttons on Shane's shirt until it hung open. She was eager to feel the warmth from his chest, hard abdomen and flat stomach underneath her fingertips. He was hot with desire for her. She reached for his belt buckle and unzipped his pants and reached inside to stroke him. He was hot, sleek, taut and ready for her. "Condom?" She looked into Shane's hazel eyes.

"Pocket," he whispered. His lips covered hers again hungrily, thrusting deep with his tongue, reminding her exactly what he intended to do with his body.

Once Gabrielle found the protection, she pushed his pants to his feet and quickly took care of protecting them.

Shane meanwhile reached for the hem of her skirt and hiked it up to her waist. He pushed her panties down her legs, and she kicked them aside and circled her legs around his waist.

"You ready, baby?" Shane lifted her off her feet and placed her atop the counter.

"Yes, please," Gabrielle murmured. "Now!"

Shane's hard length thrust against her wet opening, and he immediately found the perfect place. He pressed harder, thrusting inside her.

"Shane—" She urged him on and his tempo increased harder and faster, relentless with pulse after pulse of pure ecstasy until Gabrielle shuddered with pleasure. Shane was right behind her, growling against her neck, once, twice—and then he was still.

Shane brushed his lips across her once more, before

lowering her to the floor. They hugged each other tightly, neither ready to let go. Shane was the first to finally pull away to collect himself and redress.

Gabrielle was shocked by what had just transpired between them as she pulled down her skirt. *What had gotten into them?* They were in the office, for Christ's sake. She bent down to grab her panties strewn across the floor and threw them in her purse.

"Are you okay?" Shane asked, turning back around to face her.

"Uh, I guess," Gabrielle murmured as she rebuttoned her blouse. "What was that?"

Shane's hazel eyes peered into her brown ones. "I think we both know *why* that happened. We were hungry for each other, and no matter how much your head may think this is not the ideal situation, your body thinks otherwise."

Gabrielle inhaled sharply. "Shane…"

"I don't want to hear that this was wrong," Shane replied. "We're both adults. Let's just see how this plays out. You know, enjoy ourselves."

"I think we just did that," Gabrielle said with a laugh.

"Yeah, that was pretty hot." Shane smiled, revealing his sparkling pearly whites. "Want to do it again?" He took a tentative step toward her, but Gabrielle held her hand out and pushed against his hard chest.

"Slow down, cowboy," Gabrielle said. "This was a one-time-only thing. We need to keep this private."

Shane put one finger underneath her chin and forced Gabrielle to look up at him. "Does that mean you're finally ready to admit you'd *like* this to happen again?"

"I think my actions today are self-explanatory," Gabrielle said, underneath hooded lashes. She was perched on a dangerous tightrope. She couldn't very well admit that she didn't want Shane, because she did. Yet, she knew things would end badly, especially considering Shane's history of being a player. *Should she go backward or forward?*

"I'm glad to hear that," Shane said, sealing his mouth to hers. "I was beginning to think I'd lost my touch."

"Well, someone finally returned my call," Courtney replied when Gabrielle showed up to brunch on Sunday at a local patisserie that Courtney liked to frequent.

"I'm sorry, Courtney," Gabrielle said. "My life has been a little crazy these days."

"Is that so?" Courtney asked, reaching for her cup of cappuccino and taking a sip. "And would I know why?"

Gabrielle smiled broadly. "Yes, it's Shane," she confirmed. "We are seeing each other."

"I knew it! Shane tried to act like nothing had happened, but I knew better."

"Everything happened as you said it would," Gabrielle gushed. "When Shane saw me a couple of weeks ago at the dinner party, he was…"

"Spellbound?" Courtney offered.

"Something like that. And one thing led to another and… Well, you know…" Gabrielle felt shy talking about sleeping with Courtney's brother.

"Ended up in bed together?" Courtney replied. "Okay, so you know Shane is not immune to you, so what's next?"

"What do you mean?"

"I mean, where do you see things going from here?"

Gabrielle shrugged. "We'll see each other, you know, date."

"Hmm…" Courtney mulled over Gabrielle's statement. "Yes, but I know my brother. And Shane gets bored after he gets what he wants. My advice will be not to give him too much. You know, remain mysterious. Shane needs a woman to challenge him."

"Oh, trust me, I'm not a pushover," Gabrielle said.

"Good," Courtney said. "Because Shane needs a woman like you."

"Thank you for coming with me today," Kayla said as she and Shane entered the hospital where they'd be attending a Lamaze class together. Ethan was out of town on a business trip and her brother had graciously agreed to come in his place as her partner.

"No problem. You know I'll always be here for you," Shane said, opening the door for her so she could enter.

"Did you remember the pillow for my butt?" Kayla asked, turning around.

Shane held up the pillow and mat that she'd asked him to carry in. "I can follow directions, sis."

"Sorry," she said and then blushed.

When they arrived at the meeting room, ten other couples were already making themselves comfortable on the floor. Shane spread out the mat and placed the pillow on top and helped Kayla to the floor.

Shane glanced around. This was all kind of surreal for him, being surrounded by so many pregnant women.

"Are you okay?" Kayla asked when she saw the nervous expression on Shane's face. "It's not like you're the father, you know."

Shane laughed shakily. "I know that."

"You're my pretend daddy for today."

"Are you comfortable?" Shane asked, lowering himself to the floor and scooting behind her as he saw several other men doing.

"I am," Kayla said, leaning back against him for support. "So before class starts, why don't you tell me what's been going on with you."

"Everything's going rather nicely."

"So does that mean you're seeing Gabrielle Burton?" Kayla inquired.

"And if I were?" Shane asked. Although Kay was his sister, she was also officially his boss and might frown on a workplace romance.

Kayla didn't answer because the instructor clapped her hands to signal class was to begin.

"To prepare for labor and contractions takes patience and training," the instructor began. "Studies show that your birth experience will be much easier and shorter if you use relaxation techniques. Our goal is to show you those techniques and help you practice."

She walked over to the light switch and dimmed the lights.

"Today we are going to work on some breathing and massage techniques. I want you to focus on deep breathing through your nose," she said.

Kayla lightly reclined her head and breathed in deeply and out again. "And if you were seeing Gabrielle, I would advise you to be careful."

"You're supposed to be breathing," Shane whispered in her ear.

"I can multitask," Kayla responded. "I do run an international cosmetics company."

The instructor came over to them and placed her forefinger to her mouth to silence them. "As the partner, your role is to keep the mother calm and relaxed." She gave Shane the evil eye. "And to be encouraging."

"Did you see that?" Shane whispered. "She doesn't think I'm being encouraging and keeping you calm. You're the one who brought up my relationship."

"You mean your affair," Kayla said with her eyes closed as she half attempted her breathing exercises. "You know you never stay with one woman longer than a few months. What happens after?"

"We are both adults, Kay."

"Yes, but whenever sex is involved, emotions always come. I'm a woman. Trust me, I know these things."

"Well, trust me that I have this covered," Shane replied. "Now lie back and do as I say."

Kayla peeked up at him with one eye open. "You do realize this is the only time you'll get to boss me around? I am your boss and your big sister."

"Yeah, yeah, yeah." Shane laughed.

Chapter 8

"What do you say to dinner and a show tonight?" Shane asked one evening after work, a couple of weeks later. They had just finished collaborating on the scents for the new shower gels and lotions and had come to an agreement. Shane had really started listening to her ideas. He respected her opinion and was treating her as an equal.

"Do you think that's wise?" Gabrielle asked. They'd pretty much kept their relationship restricted to a casual hookup after work at her hotel room, watching a movie or grabbing a bite to eat in some obscure part of town. This would be their first foray out in public.

"Well, if we were to run into anyone I can say that I scored these tickets from my sister," Shane replied, "which would be the truth." Courtney had to go on an unexpected business trip and had given him the tickets.

Gabrielle's face split into a wide grin. "Then I would love it."

"Okay, then." Shane gave her a warm smile that was just as intimate as a kiss. "Why don't you head out early and I'll pick you up at six."

Shane arrived promptly at Gabrielle's door at 6:00 p.m. She had just enough time to shower, flat-iron her hair until it was silky smooth to her shoulders and slide on the evening dress she'd borrowed from the fashion department. Like Courtney, she was a size four, and the shimmering metallic loaner gown fit perfectly. It had a single ruched seam and cascading ruffle down the front that defined the languid, drapey fit of the dress with its single long sleeve and front slit.

"You look hot!" Shane commented when Gabrielle opened the door.

"So do you." Shane was wearing a modern tuxedo with a two-button jacket with a satin lapel and flat-front trousers that showed off his trim waist.

"Thank you. You ready to go?" Shane asked. "The show starts at 8:00 p.m. and I thought we could grab a prix fixe dinner on the way."

"Sounds great!" Gabrielle grabbed her clutch purse and they were out the door.

A fifteen-minute ride later and they were at an Italian restaurant filled with the theater crowd coming for dinner before a show. The meal of grilled chicken and butternut squash risotto was divine, but Gabrielle hardly noticed. Although she appreciated her privacy, she was excited to be with Shane out in the open. No hiding or sneaking around; they were finally out in public for the whole world to see. She felt confident standing next to Shane, and not just because she'd had a makeover. It was because he looked at her as if she was the only woman in the room. They shared a lively discussion about politics, the Atlanta

Braves and of course what dessert they wanted to share. They settled on the tiramisu.

Gabrielle thoroughly enjoyed the show, and not just because of its talented stars. Shane had held her hand for the majority of the night and never let go. When the evening was over, they walked hand in hand back to his Jaguar, where he surprised her by inviting her back to his place.

Gabrielle's eyes grew large. "What will your parents think?" She barely knew his parents, other than a cursory introduction at their party. She didn't want to give them the impression that she was some sort of brazen hussy.

"Not the family estate, silly," Shane said and laughed. "My loft."

"You have your own place?"

"Heck, yeah!" Shane responded. "I love my family and we're very close, but sometimes I do need my privacy, if you know what I mean."

As his gaze came to study her face, there was an invitation lying in the smoldering depths of his eyes. "I do."

"Then, let's go." Shane eagerly grabbed her hand. Gabrielle had no doubt Shane would deliver on every delectable promise in those liquid eyes of his. And hours later, he had.

"I'd like you both to go to Paris," Ethan said to Shane and Gabrielle at the development meeting a week later. "Gerard Devereux has created another great design, and the bottle prototype would be great for Ecstasy. However…"

"He doesn't want to sell to you?" Shane finished. "Why am I not surprised?"

"Yes." Ethan should have known Shane would know the man. "He's hesitant to work with large companies like Graham International."

"We need you to go over and personally speak with Gerard," Kayla added. "Let him know that although we're now part of a large conglomerate like GI, we are still a small company at heart."

"We're on it," Shane said, smiling across the table at Gabrielle. He hadn't been back to Paris in several years and going with Gabby would be even more fun.

"Don't come back until you have the design in hand," Kayla said, smiling.

"You should know me by now," Shane said. "I'm persuasive and I never give up."

"This is exciting. I get to see everything from the ground up..." Gabrielle said from the couch at Shane's loft in the city later that evening. Ever since he'd surprised her by taking her back to his place a week ago after the show, she'd gotten accustomed to spending time there.

Shane's industrial-style warehouse loft had a twelve-foot ceiling and ten-foot windows. There were funky cement columns and exposed ducts and brick walls throughout the loft. Gabrielle liked the open layout, maple hardwood floors and the large windows that allowed for lots of natural sunlight. It didn't surprise her that Shane had opted for the best with a state-of-the-art gourmet kitchen and a vast living room with a mounted fifty-inch TV and surround-sound system.

"Haven't you been involved in product development before?" Shane asked as they sat around the limestone wood-burning fireplace drinking cabernet.

"Yes," Gabrielle said with a nod. "I sat in on the meetings, but it was all pretty much a foregone conclusion at that point. All the decisions had already been made, and I rarely had much input once my products became a reality."

"AC is different. Although our reach is farther now thanks to GI's distribution, we operate much the same as we did, like a small company with Ethan and Kayla having equal power."

"I'm sure the Graham International board must love that," Gabrielle commented.

"Probably not," Shane conceded. "But it seems to work, and it saved Ethan and Kayla's marriage. Enough about business," he said, pulling her toward him. He took the wineglass out of her hand and set it on the coffee table. "I'm looking forward to having you all to myself in the 'City of Love.'"

Shane watched her pupils widen and her lips part, just as he swayed forward to press his lips against hers. Her soft, cool hands cupped his face and she slanted her lips more firmly over his. A hot ache grew inside him at having complete access to her lips. He demanded a response and Gabby freely gave it. Oh, yes, Paris was going to be fun indeed.

The overnight flight to Paris was long for Shane, but having Gabby by his side more than made up for it. During the night, he'd found Gabby snuggled next to him with her head on his shoulder. Shane had felt an inexplicable need to take care of her and had pulled the blanket up to her shoulders and nestled her closer to him. They'd been seeing each other only a month or so, but he was enjoying her company immensely.

He'd discovered that Gabrielle had a wicked sense of humor that he hadn't expected at first glance. He'd thought she was cold and aloof, but it was because he didn't know her. He knew her now. He knew that she was a morning person and liked to get in an early run. He knew that she preferred to eat one thing at a time before moving on to the next dish. The only thing he knew very little about was her family.

For some reason or another, Gabby never mentioned her family. She'd indicated she'd *had* a brother, which Shane surmised meant he was deceased. But her parents, she was closemouthed about. Shane took it to mean she wasn't close to them, so he didn't push. When she was ready, she would reveal all.

"We're here," Gabrielle said, breaking Shane out of his reverie. It was morning and the hired car he'd arranged for had stopped in front of their hotel. Gabrielle jumped out before Shane could come around and open her door. The hotel was situated directly across from the Tuileries Gardens.

She was stunned by the hotel. The exterior was classic French architecture. She'd heard of the hotel before but never had the pleasure of staying there.

Shane exited from the other side and walked around to look at the hotel. "You like?" He'd spared no expense. He'd told Kayla not to worry about expensing this trip. He would make the travel arrangements himself because he had just the hotel in mind.

"Welcome to the Le Meurice," the hotel bellman said, opening the door to the hotel.

The inside was like a French palace, with marble, gold-leafed white columns, chandeliers, gilded chairs and beautiful draperies.

"Did AC approve this?" Gabrielle asked from Shane's side.

"No, this is all me." Shane squeezed her hand. "I wanted it to be special."

They checked in and soon they were on their way via private elevator to the seventh floor and the Belle Étoile Royal Suite. A butler greeted them at the door and showed them around the light and airy suite, which housed a sitting room, dining room and master bedroom with a bathroom made of Italian marble.

"Let me show you the best feature of this room." The butler motioned for them to follow him and led them out to a private terrace.

"Wow!" Gabrielle exclaimed. She could see Notre Dame, the Arc de Triomphe and the Eiffel Tower from any area on the terrace.

"Did I do good?" Shane asked, watching Gabby's excited expression.

"This is really quite lovely. I'm touched." Gabrielle smiled, before turning back around to take in the view.

"You also have a personal chef at your disposal, Mr. Adams," the butler continued from behind them, "for anything you might desire during your stay."

"Excellent! Thank you."

"I will take my leave then?"

"Absolutely," Shane said. Once the butler left, Shane slid his arms around Gabrielle and rested his chin on her shoulder. "How about we freshen up? Go see some sights and then have some dinner. Our meeting with Gerard isn't until tomorrow."

"Sounds great!"

After they'd showered and washed off the flight, Shane and Gabrielle hit the town. They started across the street at the Tuileries Gardens, just walking around and enjoying the spring day. Then, they hailed a cab and headed to the Champs Elysées, one of Gabrielle's favorite places with its beauty and elegance, luxurious shops, theaters and famous restaurants. There was something about the wide footpaths full of Parisians and tourists that appealed to her.

She and Shane meandered through several shops and

she tried on several outfits, which Shane graciously bought for her. Now that she'd liberated herself from browns and grays, she was embracing showing off her figure in bright colors. Thanks to Shane and Courtney, she now had an entirely new stylish wardrobe.

When they reached a good spot near the end of the Champs Elysées, they took a picture with the Arc de Triomphe as the backdrop. Having lived there for the past decade, Gabrielle felt like a tourist, but she indulged Shane.

Eventually, they settled on a quiet, unassuming French bistro for dinner, where they enjoyed a four-course champagne meal. The entrée was a delicious burgundy beef dish with truffle mashed potatoes and spring vegetables that had Shane very nearly licking his plate.

After dinner, they headed back to the hotel and ended up sharing a glass of ice wine on the terrace while enjoying the 180-degree night view of the famous Paris monuments.

"Aren't the stars beautiful tonight?" Gabrielle asked, looking up at the sky as she leaned her head back against Shane's shoulders. The spicy scent of his aftershave sent her mind swirling to the last time they'd been together at his loft. The fire he'd stirred in her then was simmering now and just waiting to be rekindled.

"They're not as beautiful as you are," Shane said huskily as he massaged her shoulders.

Gabrielle heard the arousal in Shane's voice and turned around to face him. His steady gaze was riveted on her face, then moved slowly over her body and back up.

His eyes were flaming hot and Gabrielle swayed forward. Shane's arms quickly wrapped around her, bringing her closer to his masculine frame. She looped her arms around his neck and opened herself to him. His lips were warm and sweet on hers, with a promise of more to come. Gabrielle had never felt this way about a man before. She literally ached to be with Shane. He had a way of speaking to everything woman in her. The warm sweep of his tongue inside her mouth nearly caused her to swoon. His fingers combed and massaged through her hair as he seduced her with his lips.

She pressed closer to him, eager for more contact. The hard length of him told Gabrielle that Shane wanted her just as much as she wanted him. She clawed at the fastenings on his dress shirt as hunger gnawed inside her. When his muscled chest was bare to her admiring gaze, Gabrielle spread her hands over his shoulders and flicked aside the offending shirt. Shane had a beautiful, well-toned body, and Gabrielle bent down and placed butterfly kisses over his honed chest. She trailed a path down to his six-pack abs. She glanced up at him devilishly as her fingers fell to his zipper. She made fast work of relieving him from his pants, but not before reaching in his pocket and grabbing protection that she knew he kept handy for spontaneous occasions like this.

Shane stepped out of his pants and briefs until he was wearing nothing but a smile. He loved the fact that Gabrielle was taking control. When she pushed him back toward a nearby lounger on the terrace, he didn't object. Instead, he leaned back and watched her slowly unzip the spaghetti-strap cocktail dress she was wearing until she wore nothing but a champagne-colored satin bra and matching panties. Blood was pounding in his head, and his heart nearly leaped out of his chest at the sight of her exposing every inch of herself to him in such a public place as the terrace. And although no one could see them on the top floor, he loved that she was letting go of her inhibitions with him.

"Aren't you still a little overdressed?" Shane asked, glancing up at Gabrielle. He wanted to reach behind her to unsnap her bra so he could taste her breasts.

"Hmm… Someone's impatient!"

"Only when it comes to you, baby," Shane said and smiled wickedly.

Gabrielle wasn't nervous as she undressed in front of Shane. She liked his appreciative male gaze when she unhooked her bra and it, along with her panties, fell to the floor. She came toward Shane and straddled him with the condom between her teeth. It was sexy as hell, and Shane thought he was about to come right then.

"Are you going to put it on me?" he inquired.

"Wait for it," she whispered in his ear, placing the protection next to him on the lounger. Gabrielle could see he was as turned on as she was by this exercise, and she wanted to continue. "Do you always have to be in control?"

"No, I don't. What do you have in mind?"

Gabrielle nipped at his front jaw first and then buried her face in his neck, tasting and nibbling while her hands fanned over his chest, lightly teasing his nipples with her fingertips.

A groan grumbled from deep within Shane, and he went to cup her hips and full behind, but Gabrielle smacked his hands way. "God, woman, you're not playing fair."

"In due time," Gabrielle replied. She dipped her head and flicked her tongue over a nipple. She lavished it and the other with equal attention before drawing circles over his stomach as she made her way lower. She continued to trace lower until she reached his hard arousal. She stroked him, slowly and deliberately, until she felt Shane contract at her touch, and that's when she replaced her hands with her warm mouth. Shane's eyes slammed shut, his teeth clenched and he grabbed a handful of her hair in his hands.

"Gabby... Oh, Gabby..." he hissed.

Gabrielle shifted and fluidly smoothed a condom down his arousal. She didn't want him to come without her, but she also wanted to try something new. And with Shane she felt as if she could. Quickly, she spun herself around so her back was to Shane and carefully guided his penis until she felt the thick pressure of him inside of her.

"Gabby, you naughty girl," Shane said from behind her as he reached around to stroke her breasts, belly and thighs. Using her feet and legs as leverage, Gabrielle moved up and down Shane's penis, savoring the sensual feeling and stimulation.

"Yes, baby." Shane kissed and caressed her shoulders, back and spine. He loved watching her wiggle her tight butt from side to side—it made him even hornier.

He was surprised when Gabby leaned her body back as lightly and softly as a feather, and her upper body sank into his chest. And when Gabby tightened her muscles around him, Shane felt pleasurable contractions spread throughout his entire body. He reached down and lightly stroked the wet lips of her womanhood until he came to her clitoris. When he did, he stimulated it with gentle flicks until Gabrielle cried out.

"Shane!"

She was on the edge, and Shane knew it. He flipped positions quickly so that Gabrielle was beneath him. With her legs over his shoulders, he thrust full and deep inside her. The sweet scent of jasmine in her perfume wafted through his nose, arousing him even more. He slid two fingers between them and teased at Gabby's taut nub that was a bundle of raw nerves. Gabrielle moaned aloud as pulsations rocked through her very core.

Shane gripped her hips harder and thrust one final time as pure bliss took over his entire body. He sagged over her and their sweat-slicked bodies were skin-to-skin. Shane stroked her hair and placed a moist kiss on her forehead as he eased onto his side. Gabrielle could barely glance up at Shane because she was overwhelmed. She was completely fulfilled and also in way over her head. She couldn't forget her fear that this dalliance with Shane would end badly.

He had made such an impact on her life in such a short amount of time. *Would she be able to handle it when Shane inevitably wanted to move on to the next woman?*

Chapter 9

"This glasswork you've done is simply stunning, Gerard," Shane said the following morning at the glassmaker's small shop in the heart of Paris.

The cobalt-blue of the crystal glass and the angular shape made the bottle stylish and sophisticated. It was exactly what Shane was looking for for Ecstasy.

"Thank you, Shane," Gerard replied. "And this scent that you made is really quite lovely." Shane had allowed him to smell a sample.

"Thank you, but it was a team effort." Shane smiled and glanced at Gabrielle.

She appreciated that he wasn't one of those bosses who didn't give credit where credit was due. He appreciated her comments on some of the notes in the fragrance and wasn't afraid to say so. In the short time they'd been working together, Shane had made a complete transformation as a boss. He was a changed man and more open to her opinions and ideas than he'd been when she'd started.

"But you know I can't and won't sell to a large conglomerate like Graham International," Gerard said. "You know how I feel about big business. I mean, Ethan Graham wants me to sign a long-term, exclusive agreement with him."

"I know you believe in the little guy," Shane said, taking a seat on the stool opposite Gerard while Gabrielle stood nearby and watched him work his signature charm. "And that hasn't changed."

"How can you say that with a straight face, Shane? You know everything has changed. Adams Cosmetics is now part of an international conglomerate," Gerard replied. "I thought Kayla would never sell. I thought she would go to her grave before she let that happen."

Shane remembered the exact conversation he, Kayla and Gerard had had long before Ethan entered the picture. They'd discussed the future of AC and knew that developing a fragrance was a natural progression, but then finances had run short. They'd had to put it on hold until last year, when they were forced into action to save AC. And in the end they still ended up merging with Graham International.

"Gerard." Shane walked toward the older man. He wasn't going to lie; he was going to give it to him straight. "Yes, AC is still part of GI, but at the heart, at the center of, it is still *my family*. Adamses run this company. We are the talent, the vision and the creative force behind this company. Without us there is no Adams Cosmetics, and Ethan knows it. Your bottles are exquisite masterpieces that deserve to be on display for the world to see, and what better way than by housing one of my signature fragrances?"

"Shane." Gerard sighed.

Shane knew Gerard was on the fence and gave him the final push. "How about we agree to purchase your designs on a case-by-case basis? We buy this design and you retain your rights to work with whomever you choose? This will allow you to see how AC is working as part of Graham International. What do you say?"

Gerard shook his head. "That sounds good, but Graham is never going to agree to that."

Shane smiled. "You let me handle Ethan."

"Are you sure about this?" Gabrielle asked in the car on the way back to the hotel from Gerard's office. "Ethan wanted an exclusive."

"Of course I am," Shane said emphatically. "Ethan can't get what he wants every time, and he's going to have to accept that."

"As long as you're sure," Gabrielle said, reaching over to grab his hand. "Then I'm with you."

"Trust me, it'll be fine."

Since Shane had arranged their visit to make a long weekend, they spent the next couple of days acting like tourists. They strolled through the streets of Montmartre near Sacré-Coeur. Since they'd both already seen the white-domed church, they opted to act like locals. They had crepes at one of Gabrielle's favorite spots, browsed through the local street-artists' stands and Shane even sat for a caricature portrait that Gabrielle secretly vowed to keep with her forever, even after their affair ended. They finished off the night at the Moulin Rouge. Although she'd seen the show in Montmartre half a dozen times, she acquiesced to Shane's desire to see the cancan girls and their cabaret show.

On their final day in Paris, they visited the Louvre to

see the *Mona Lisa* and several other great works of art, Notre Dame to admire its Gothic style and its stained-glass window and then took a cruise on the Seine River.

They were back in the hotel to change for dinner and Gabrielle was brushing her hair into soft waves when Shane came up behind her, admiring her in the mirror.

"Hey, you." She smiled. This had been a beautiful get-away and one she'd enjoyed immensely. It was amazing how much more romantic Paris could be when you had someone to share it with. Outside of a few friends like Mariah, she'd always been alone. She'd hoped Mariah would be able to meet Shane, but she was out of town on a photo shoot.

"You look beautiful." Shane twirled her around so he could have a better look. Gabrielle was wearing an off-the-shoulder dress of crinkled iris silk with a defined waist, and her hair was swept in a loose French roll. She looked stunning.

"You'd look even better with this." Shane slid a platinum teardrop pendant necklace around her neck.

"Shane, what's this?" Gabrielle asked, fingering the beautiful gift. Although to some it might seem like a simple gift, it meant everything to her that Shane knew just the kind of thing she would wear.

"Just a little something to remember me by."

"You didn't have to do that." Gabrielle doubted she would have any problems remembering Shane. Snapshots of them making love in the multijet shower this morning or the enormous marble whirlpool bathtub they'd shared two nights ago flashed in her mind. Oh, yes… Gabrielle would have a *hard time* forgetting Shane.

"I wanted to," Shane said, stroking her cheek. "C'mon, I have something special planned for our last night in Paris."

A chauffeured car took them the short trip from their

hotel to the Eiffel Tower. Shane exited the vehicle first and came around to help Gabrielle out, wrapping her arm around his.

"Are we having dinner here?" Gabrielle asked, looking up at the Eiffel Tower in all of its brilliant splendor. She loved the way the tower was all lit up at night.

"I know it might seem a little cliché, but when in Paris…" Shane said, walking toward the entrance of the tower.

A short elevator ride later, they arrived at the Le Jules Verne restaurant, and the view offered them the entire city of Paris at their feet. The maître d' sat them in a secluded alcove, and they feasted on a contemporary Parisian prix fixe meal, starting off with escargot and ending with a cherry soufflé.

Afterward, Shane hated to see the evening end, but they had to get back to the States. He'd already extended the trip to give them some alone time. But the more time he spent with Gabby, the more he wanted to be with her. He already knew they worked well together in the lab and in the bedroom, but this long weekend had been different. He'd discovered new facets of Gabrielle—that she liked museums and art, but didn't care to spend her entire afternoon there. And unlike most women, she didn't enjoy clothes and shoes, but she loved collecting handbags. They'd stopped at a half dozen stores, so she could see what was new in the shops. She'd even surprised him at the Moulin Rouge, when a couple of the cancan girls asked for people onstage and she volunteered. He'd loved seeing her shake her hips onstage and when her eyes had connected with his, it had been as if she was dancing only for him.

It was hard to find anything he didn't like about Gabrielle. It scared him at first, but he tried to chalk it up to the early stages of infatuation. Once he got her out of his system, he would move on to the next woman.

"What do you say we get out of here?" Shane asked.

"Not without going to the top and taking a picture!"

Several photographs later, with the city of Paris as their backdrop, they were back in the car and headed back to the Le Meurice's royal suite.

Shane was a generous lover that night, making sure Gabrielle's every need was taken care of. He'd slowly undressed her, taking time to place tiny, nibbling kisses all over her body. When she was naked, he'd pushed her back to the bed and she'd watched as he removed his clothes with as much finesse as was possible, seeing that his erection had been pressing hard against her when he'd kissed her.

Nobody she'd ever been with had ever made her feel weak at the knees, but that's exactly how Shane made her feel with every stroke of his tongue on her lips, inside her mouth, between her breasts. When he reached the dusky nipples and sucked hard, Gabrielle grabbed fistfuls of his hair and urged him on.

"I'm going to enjoy every single inch of you," Shane murmured. He rocked back on his haunches and gave her a wicked grin before he lowered himself between her thighs. He took his time, idling his way along her thighs before finally coming to her sex. He gently nuzzled her womanly lips and then she felt the moist stroke of his tongue working its way around her before finally coming to her clitoris. He gave her exactly what she wanted by varying the rhythm and flicking his tongue from side to side. Gabby opened up to him like a flower in the morning sun. He knew the moment she climaxed because she arched off the bed and babbled his name. Shane tongued her further and soon she was having another orgasm.

Time blurred for Gabrielle, and she closed her eyes, eager for the pleasure to continue. She didn't realize Shane was poised above her until she felt the tip of his penis at her entrance, pressing forward.

He felt so good and so right that she easily accepted him. He began moving inside her, in and out, in and out, driving them both mad. He jammed his mouth over hers, kissing her hard and bringing them both to a tumultuous climax that had Shane shouting and Gabrielle crying out.

Afterward, Shane held her close and stroked her hair. "That was truly beautiful, Gabby." He tangled his fingers inside her now-damp curls and stole another kiss.

"I know," she whispered.

Chapter 10

"You didn't get Gerard to sign the exclusive contract?" Kayla asked when Shane walked into her office on Monday afternoon.

"No." Shane was in no mood for a go-around with his sister. He'd only intended to come into the lab to check on things when he'd been summoned to his sister's office. He'd had very little sleep on the plane, and then he hadn't been able to sleep at the loft. *Had it been because Gabrielle wasn't there?* She'd said she had to take care of some personal business, and so he'd had to spend the night alone. He hadn't realized he was getting used to having her in his bed until she wasn't there.

"Well, why not?" Kayla asked. "Was that not your express purpose in going?"

"My *express purpose*," Shane returned, "was to get the prototype and the design of the bottle that Gerard created.

Getting him to sign that exclusive agreement was secondary. And I have the prototype." He held the bottle up in his hand.

Shane leaned over the desk and handed it to her. "This is great, Shane. It's vibrant and eye-catching, even more so in person than the photographs. Add your delicious scent and consumers will go wild for this."

"I know, Kay, which is why I wasn't about to push Gerard."

Kayla nodded. "Ethan still isn't going to be happy about this. He doesn't want other companies to find out about Gerard and snatch him up."

"Gerard is his own man. He will never work with a huge conglomerate. Trust me."

"Well, I guess we're going to have to bank on your gut instincts," Kayla snapped.

"Why did that sound like a dig?" Shane asked. "Have I ever steered this company wrong before?"

"Of course not. And I'm sorry, Shane. I'm just a little hormonal these days. This little one has been keeping me up nights, either kicking or giving me heartburn."

"I hear you. I didn't get much sleep myself last night."

Kayla raised a brow. "Oh, really. Was that because Gabrielle was over?"

"Kayla!"

"C'mon, you didn't really think I was that daft, did you?" she asked. "When you want something or *someone,* you usually go after it. And you wanted Gabby. Plus, Courtney filled me in on everything."

Shane rolled his eyes upward. "Our little sister is a gossip and needs to mind her own business."

"True, but we know she never will. You remember how she was about Ethan?"

Shane laughed. "I do, but she had a good reason. Dad hated his guts."

"And Gabby is your employee, which could complicate the situation."

"There *is* that." Shane nodded in agreement. "Listen, I have to get going, but I'm going to put this—" he reached for the prototype "—in the lab safe until marketing is ready."

"Jax Cosmetics won't know what hit them."

"They sure won't."

Gabrielle was shocked when she'd turned on her phone during the layover from Paris and heard a message from her father. She'd thought he would have gotten the message that she wasn't about to do his or Andrew Jackson's dirty business.

She'd returned the call only to tell him where to go, but he'd been apologetic and asked if he could see her when she returned. She'd decided not to spend the evening in Shane's arms, where she would have liked to have been, because visiting her parents would take a lot out of her mentally and she needed the night to regroup after a long flight.

Shane had generously given her the day off. She would have liked nothing better than to be at work instead of meeting with her father, but she'd agreed to see him anyway.

"Daddy, why are you here?" she asked when he came to her apartment that afternoon.

"Nice digs," he commented, glancing around her fully furnished one-bedroom apartment. She'd liked the apartment because of the arched doorways, track lighting, deluxe crown moldings and ceramic-tile floor. It also came with a gourmet stainless-steel kitchen and a garden bathtub, which was her favorite feature.

She'd found the place a couple of weeks ago, and just

in the nick of time because the hotel was becoming expensive. She'd arranged for the rest of her belongings to be shipped from Paris, and the boxes were now stacked up neatly against the wall.

"Thanks, but I'm sure you're not here to comment on my decor. So why did you come?"

"I tried calling you the last few days. Where were you?" he asked.

"I was in Paris."

"You thinking of going back?" he asked. "I thought you were finally home to stay."

"I was there on business."

"For Adams Cosmetics?"

"Yes, Daddy, for my employer. And if you're here to call me a traitor, you can leave, because I won't be berated for doing the right thing. What you asked me to do was wrong. Just plain wrong."

"I know that, baby girl. That's why I'm here."

"You are?" Gabrielle was shocked.

"I'm here because I wanted to apologize for asking you to bail me out. You didn't get me into this mess. I did."

A lump formed in Gabrielle's throat, and she wanted to swallow but couldn't. "Thank you."

"I'm going to get me some help."

"I think that's a great idea." Tears sprang to her eyes. If he was ready to recognize he had a problem, then she was willing to support him. "And I can help. Give me a minute." She briefly left the room to get her checkbook. When she returned, her father was standing by the window near her briefcase. Her briefcase held all her important papers from her Paris trip, including a picture of Gerard's bottle for Ecstasy, but her father would never search through her things.

"Daddy?"

Her father glanced up, but his eyes barely met hers. "Yeah?"

"I can help get you into a good rehab program, and you wouldn't have to worry about the cost. I would take care of it."

"Uh, that's not necessary." He looked down. "Um… We can mortgage the house to, you know, to pay off the debts."

"Are you sure?" Gabrielle asked. "I may not be able to help you in the way you wanted, but I can certainly help you get clean."

"Yeah… I'm sure. Uh… Listen…that's all I came to say," her father said, shifting nervously from one foot to the other.

"Okay." Gabrielle attempted a smile. "I'm so glad you came."

Her father paused, as if looking for his words. But instead of speaking, he came over and gave her a quick hug and then rushed out, leaving the door open.

Gabrielle was stunned by the tiny act of affection and burst into tears. She couldn't remember the last time one of her parents had hugged her, much less said they loved her. She hadn't realized just how much she needed it or them until now.

Shane was distracted. He had already messed up several experiments in the lab before finally deciding it was time to call it quits for the day. He handed the experiments over to one of the other chemists and hopped into his Jaguar.

He hadn't been able to get Gabby out of his head all day. Even though they maintained their professionalism in the lab, he always knew Gabrielle was there, but today he'd felt disconcerted because she wasn't there. And he'd gotten used to having her around. He missed her.

Before he knew it, he was driving to Gabrielle's apartment. He was surprised to find the door to her apartment slightly ajar. He was instantly concerned, and when he heard crying, his heart stopped. *Was she okay? Was she hurt? Injured?*

"Gabby?" Shane asked, walking inside and closing the door. The living room was empty, but he could still hear sobs. He followed the direction of the sounds and found her lying on the side of her bed. "Gabby?" he asked, coming to squat in front of her. He brushed away her hair and saw her tearstained cheeks and red eyes and immediately wanted to the beat the crap out of whoever had hurt her. "What's wrong, baby? What happened?"

Gabrielle merely shook her head. She couldn't speak. Her family, the situation, was all too much.

Shane rose and scooted beside her on the bed, pulling her into his arms. Gabrielle circled her arms around his waist and just cried. It was hard for him to see her in that much pain and not know how to alleviate it.

When she finally quieted, he asked, "What can I do?"

She was quiet for a long moment and Shane wondered if she'd heard him, but she finally whispered against his chest, "Exactly what you're doing."

They lay in bed together for a long time with Shane just holding her. Eventually Gabrielle was calm enough to finally talk, so Shane pushed the pillows behind her and she sat up. "Better now?" he asked.

His gaze was focused so intently on Gabrielle, and she felt embarrassed. "Yeah. Sorry about that."

"There's no need to be sorry."

"I guess I didn't realize how much I've been holding in."

"Did something happen when we got back?"

Gabrielle shook her head.

"Before?"

Gabrielle nodded. "It's my parents, we haven't been close since…since…"

Shane's large, masculine hand covered hers. "If you don't want to talk about it, you don't have to."

"Maybe that's the problem. I haven't talked about it and it's been eating me up inside." Gabrielle swallowed several times and finally told Shane what she had never told anyone. "My parents and I haven't been close since my brother, Seth, died. They blamed me for his death…. Because he died saving me from drowning and he… He ended up drowning himself."

"Oh, God, Gabby, that's terrible." Shane was stunned by the revelation. "How old were you?"

"I… I was fifteen and my brother was seventeen. Seth was my big brother and the light of my life. It hurt me as much as it hurt them, but they could only see their own pain. They never comforted me; they never hugged me after he died. It was as if I died too right along with him. We've been estranged ever since then, which is why I stayed in Paris after school. And today, out of the blue, my dad hugged me. After all this time…"

"Shh, it's okay." Shane gathered her in his arms and stroked her hair. "It's okay."

"We've been at odds since I got back, so it was just so unexpected…"

"And long overdue." Shane wished Gabby could have had the happy family life he had growing up. He wished he could take away all the pain that she'd ever felt or still felt, but he couldn't. "But whenever you need a hug—" Shane squeezed her tighter in his arms "—you just let me know."

Gabrielle wanted it to be true, wanted to know she could rely on Shane, but deep down she knew it was a passing fancy, and that one day, one day soon, she would have to let go. But for now, she basked in the knowledge that, at that moment, Shane wanted to be with her and no one else.

"What?" Shane yelled from his office door a couple of days later. Everyone in the lab looked up.

Gabrielle was stunned by Shane's outburst and watched him come barreling out of his office. "Is something wrong?"

Shane didn't answer. "Gabrielle, come with me, please."

Gabrielle dropped what she was doing and immediately followed behind him. "Where are we going?"

"Emergency meeting," Shane said, slamming through the lab's double doors.

Gabrielle trotted to keep up with his long, purposeful strides. He was silent on the elevator ride up to the executive floor. She tried to read his expression and could tell that whatever had happened was dire, because his eyes were cloudy and unreadable. When they made it to the conference room, Ethan, Kayla, Courtney and several marketing executives were already gathered.

"Close the door," Ethan spit out. Gabrielle knew it was bad. She watched Shane take a deep breath but do as requested. They both took a seat at the long table, and Gabrielle ended up next to Courtney.

"You want to tell me how the hell something like this happened?" Ethan yelled, his wrath directed squarely at Shane.

Shane's eyes narrowed when he spoke. "I don't know."

"That's unacceptable, Shane."

"What's going on?" Gabrielle whispered to Courtney.

"The design for the bottle was leaked on the internet," Courtney replied.

"What?" A sinking feeling came over Gabrielle. She'd had several photos of the prototype in her briefcase at her apartment. And her father had been there a few days ago. *Could he have looked in her briefcase?*

"When I got back, after showing Kayla, I immediately put the prototype in the safe," Gabrielle heard Shane say, but she was too distracted by the fear that was coursing through her veins to focus. *Would her father have gone that far for Andrew Jackson? Would he have acted sincere and hugged her if he hadn't meant it?*

"Then how was it leaked?

"Why don't you tell me?" Shane hissed. "You're the one with the top-notch security, Ethan. Why don't you tell me how someone could get in the safe?"

"Did it ever leave your possession in Paris?" Kayla inquired, trying to avert an explosive situation. But Shane shook his head. He'd ensured the prototype was locked in the hotel safe.

"What about Gerard?" Ethan replied, rising from his chair. "He didn't want to sign an exclusive... Perhaps he wanted more money?"

"It wasn't Gerard," Shane stated emphatically.

"How can you be sure?" Ethan stood over Shane and glared at him.

"Because I know him," Shane said, looking up at his brother-in-law without batting an eye.

"And I thought I knew you," Ethan replied. "I trusted you with this and you dropped the ball."

"Ethan..." There was a warning tone in Kayla's voice. She did not care for his accusatory tone.

Ethan glanced at his wife and then returned to his seat. "Clearly, security needs to be beefed up. In the meantime, I need you—" he turned to his publicity and marketing executives "—to do damage control. We need to get control of this situation. We can't let Ecstasy's launch be damaged by this leak."

Several executives nodded in agreement.

"Meeting adjourned," Ethan announced and everyone began filing out, with the exception of Shane, Courtney and Kayla.

Gabrielle glanced at Shane. She didn't want to leave him without backup. She knew Shane was conscientious about his work in the lab and couldn't imagine he'd made an error. And if she was responsible for this travesty, she would never forgive herself. But Shane mouthed for her to go back to the lab.

Once everyone had gone, Kayla turned to Ethan. "Was that really necessary?"

"I don't need you to fight my battles, Kay," Shane responded testily. "I am in charge of the lab, and it's my responsibility to guard our intellectual property."

"I know that," Kayla replied. "But you were right in that we need to ensure this isn't a security issue, either."

"And we will look into that," Ethan said.

"As will I." Shane swiftly rose from the table and left the room, causing the chair he'd been sitting in to spin out of control.

Courtney went to follow behind her brother, but Gabrielle was waiting for him. Clearly, Gabrielle had stayed behind to make sure Shane was okay, and that concerned Courtney. Shane was known for loving and leaving women, and although Courtney hoped Gabrielle was the woman to tame Shane, she also wasn't sure Gabrielle would be prepared for the fallout if their affair should end.

"Let him go," Courtney said, walking toward Gabrielle. She knew when Shane needed to blow off some steam.

Gabrielle turned around guiltily, as if her hand had been

caught in the cookie jar. "But he needs me." He'd been so furious that he hadn't even noticed her sitting in the hall.

That was a telling statement, and Courtney grabbed Gabrielle by the arm. "Come with me," she ordered and led Gabrielle into her office on the same floor.

Once inside, Courtney closed the door and leaned back against it. "You've fallen for Shane, haven't you?"

Gabrielle's eyes grew large. Courtney had her answer.

Courtney grasped her by the hand and led her to the cream leather sofa. "And Shane, how does he feel about you?"

"We haven't discussed our feelings," Gabrielle answered honestly. "I mean, I don't even know what *I'm* feeling. This is all so new to me."

"But you do have strong feelings for Shane?"

Gabrielle nodded. "I do, but I'm such a mess, Courtney. I've so much going on in my life." *That was the understatement of the year, considering her father could have very well have stolen from her!* "Perhaps I'm making more of this than it actually is…. I have always had a slight crush on Shane, so maybe that's all it is. But then again, whenever I'm around him, I get butterflies and sometimes my mouth goes dry and when he kisses me I get weak in the knees. Oh, Lord, I sound like a schoolgirl." Gabrielle put her head in her hands.

Courtney laughed. "No, you sound like a woman in love. Maybe you should try feeling Shane out to see how he feels?"

"I know how he feels. He wants me in his bed every night."

Courtney held up her hands. "Okay, T.M.I., he is still my brother." She smiled. "Seriously, though, have a talk with him and see where his head is."

"What will he say?" Gabrielle asked.

Courtney shrugged. "I don't know, but whatever he says, you'll have to decide for yourself exactly what you're willing to accept."

It was well after 5:00 p.m. when Courtney made it down to the laboratory. She had waited until everyone had left so she could speak to Shane alone. She would have tried at the mansion, but Shane had made a habit of staying at his loft in the city these days. Courtney suspected it had something to do with a certain brunette, but Shane would never admit to it.

"Hey, you," Courtney said, walking uninvited into Shane's office.

"Hey." Shane barely looked up from the papers he was reading.

"Ethan was pretty hard on you earlier."

"It was well deserved," Shane said. "The lab is my domain, which I made clear from day one when we merged with Graham International. It's just—" he sighed "—I don't know how something like this could have happened. I've been so careful."

"Don't worry," Courtney said. "We'll find the culprit. And in the meantime, we'll get some free press for Ecstasy and have the public hungering for the fragrance when it launches."

Shane couldn't help but smile. Trust his little sister to always look on the bright side. "Thanks, kid."

"So…" Courtney said, leaning forward. "How are things going with you and Gabby?"

"You mean this wasn't a professional visit?" Shane's voice rose slightly, as if he were shocked by his sister's question. But he wasn't surprised. Courtney had shown amazing restraint, considering she was the orchestrator of the relationship. She'd given him that extra boost and he'd finally seen Gabby for the beautiful, smart woman she was.

"No, it isn't."

Shane's eyebrow rose questioningly.

"I'm worried about you two."

"Worried, why? Everything is going smoothly," Shane replied. "Actually, better than that."

"That's the problem."

"How so?"

"You need to be careful with Gabby's heart, Shane," Courtney responded. "We women get easily attached after becoming intimate. Although, I would have to say I'm not one of them." Courtney was similar to her brother in that respect. She didn't want or need love. She was having too much fun living in the moment. Unlike Shane, who always seemed to need companionship, though not for the long-term.

Shane frowned. "Has Gabby said something?" *Was she starting to develop strong feelings toward him, as he was toward her?* If so, she hadn't said anything. She was good at covering up her feelings, but then again, she'd invented that art form. She'd had a lifetime of hiding her emotions from her parents. But he'd hoped that after she'd opened up to him the other day, she was beginning to feel as if she could trust him.

Courtney shook her head. She would never betray her friend's confidence, but she also didn't want Gabby to get hurt, and she knew Shane's track record.

Courtney's lack of response told Shane that perhaps there was more to the story. His little sister always had something to say, so if she was silent it meant he needed to speak with Gabby. But he had to get his sister off his back. "You needn't worry. Our relationship is strictly casual. You know I don't do long-term. Never have."

"Duly noted," Courtney said, rising from her chair and heading for the door. "I guess I should have known it's hard for a leopard to change its spots, but you be sure Gabby knows the score. I don't want her to get hurt."

"Aye, aye, captain," Shane said and saluted her.

Several seconds later, she was out the door. She didn't notice that Gabrielle had been standing behind the door and had heard their entire conversation.

Gabrielle was having a bad night. She'd tried unsuccessfully to reach her father to find out if he had anything to do with the design leaking onto the internet. Not knowing was driving her crazy. She couldn't allow Shane to take the blame for something that could have been *her* fault.

And if that hadn't been bad enough, she'd overheard Courtney and Shane openly discussing their relationship. She'd thought about walking away, because it was a private conversation between the two siblings, but then her curiosity had gotten the better of her and she'd listened in.

She wished she hadn't. Shane had made it clear to Courtney that he didn't do long-term relationships. Just like in perfumery school, in a couple of months, Shane would tire of her and move on to the next woman. She'd told herself that she just wanted to know what it was like to be one of his women and when it was over she would move on, no big deal. She was wrong.

Now she knew exactly what it was to be one of Shane's women, and she'd loved every minute of it and didn't want to give it up. But clearly Shane had other ideas. Despite the time they'd spent in Atlanta and in Paris, nothing had changed for Shane. They hadn't grown closer, as she'd thought. Instead, he seemed just as untouchable and impenetrable as he'd been in school. Gabrielle didn't know how to digest it all. She wasn't used to letting anyone get this close, but she'd opened up to Shane as she had no other. So it was a hard pill to swallow that he wasn't as affected as she by the time they'd spent talking, laughing, sharing and making love.

A knock sounded on her apartment door and when she opened it, Shane was on the other side.

"Hey, baby." Shane kissed her cheek and went to move forward, but Gabrielle held the door in her hand, not allowing him entrance. "Is something wrong? Do you have someone else in there?" he asked jokingly.

"No," Gabrielle responded, not budging. "I'm just in the middle of something, so now isn't a good time."

Shane's mouth curled into a frown. "Are you asking me to leave?" They hadn't spent a night apart in over a month. He didn't understand why Gabby didn't want to be with him. They'd just had a long romantic weekend in Paris, which he had enjoyed immensely. And if her multiple orgasms were any indication, so had she, so why the brush-off?

"If you don't mind…" Gabrielle's voice trailed off.

The look of disappointment etched across Shane's face made Gabrielle instantly regret her decision. But it was too late. Shane had already begun backing away from the door.

"Okay, then—I guess I will see you at the office tomorrow." Shane came forward for the briefest of moments to brush his lips across hers and then he was gone.

Gabrielle closed the door and sagged against it. Seconds ticked by as she fought with her mind and her heart. Her mind told her to play it safe, and that by not sleeping next to him that night, she could keep her feelings hidden. But on the other hand, in her heart, she wanted to be with him, to be close to him.

In a split-second decision, she opened the door, praying that Shane was still waiting at the elevator landing. But it was empty. He'd gone, and so Gabrielle closed her apartment door and went to bed alone.

Chapter 11

Gabrielle was on edge. She hadn't heard back from her father, and she'd left half a dozen messages at the house for him. Even her mother wasn't responding, which could only mean that her father was behind the leak to the press. He'd used her desire for a connection with him to gain access to confidential information. She needed to tell Shane what happened, but she was ashamed by how deeply she had wanted her father's embrace and affection toward her to be true. She hoped Shane would understand, but he was keeping his distance. Ever since she'd sent him away a couple of nights ago, he'd been polite and courteous to her at the office, but nothing more. Not so much as a phone call or text.

Clearly, she'd hurt his feelings by not wanting to spend time with him and by claiming she had things to do. Now Shane was giving her all the space she needed.

Courtney had called and left a message about inviting

her to an event that weekend, but Gabrielle was too embarrassed to admit that she'd listened in on Courtney's
conversation with Shane. She knew Courtney meant well,
but it had still stung.

Last night, when she'd finally gotten up the nerve to go
into Shane's office to talk after work about the leak, he'd
been on the phone and had waved her off. Gabrielle was
beginning to wonder if he had already lost interest in her.
Could his feelings have cooled that quickly?

"So what's wrong with you?" Courtney asked when she
found Shane sitting alone at the breakfast table on Friday
morning. Their parents were nowhere in sight, so they
could talk freely.

"Coffee?" their butler Victor asked, holding up the carafe.

"Love some, thanks, Vic."

Courtney eyed her brother suspiciously.

"Why would you think something is wrong?" Shane
asked, glancing up from the business section of the news-
paper.

"Could it be because I can count on one hand the
number of times you've been back to the estate the last
couple of months?" Courtney inquired.

"It was time for a change," Shane said, continuing to
read his paper.

"Is the honeymoon over already?"

Shane rolled his eyes. He didn't really care to discuss
his relationship with Gabrielle right now. He was still
smarting over the fact that she had sent him away. He
couldn't understand why she'd didn't want to be with him
when he wanted her so badly. Last night, he'd had to do
something he'd never done. Take a cold shower. *Had he
done something to upset her?* He couldn't think of anything. And then at work, she'd been standoffish and cool

toward him. Shane didn't know what to make of it and decided it was best to give her a few days' reprieve. He hoped that after the weekend, she would be ready to discuss whatever it was that was bothering her.

Shane didn't get the opportunity to follow up with Gabrielle because all hell broke loose on Monday morning. When Shane went into his office, he noticed several items on his desk were out of place. A knot formed in his gut, and he instinctively knew something was wrong. And when he went to check the safe where he kept all his formulas, he saw one was missing. And not just any formula. It was Ecstasy.

Anger coursed through him at the thought that someone had stolen his ideas, his hard work, his passion. It was unthinkable.

Gabrielle came breezing into his office. "Shane, I was hoping we could talk."

"Not now!" Shane roared.

"Shane…" Tears sprang to Gabrielle's eyes at his harsh tone and she went flying out of the room.

Shane's first reaction was to go after her. He'd never yelled at a woman before. His mama had raised him as a Southern gentleman and that just wasn't how he spoke to his woman, or any woman. But he had more important matters on his hands. Namely, finding out *who* had stolen his scent. And then the unwelcome scene of telling Ethan and Kayla of the theft.

Neither was too happy to hear the news when Shane called a meeting in Kayla's office. "How could this have happened?" Ethan yelled. "What the hell is going on in that lab?"

"Ethan," Kayla said then breathed in deeply, "yelling will not get us anywhere."

"This is a catastrophe, Kayla, and you damn well know it."

"Don't you think I know that?" Shane yelled back at Ethan. "This is *my work* that's been stolen!"

"And it's *my money* and *my company* that's putting up the backing for this venture," Ethan responded. "We've already put so much time and effort into promoting Ecstasy. What are we going to say when it's time to debut it?"

"The thief may have major notes in the fragrance," Shane replied, "but they don't have all the pieces. It's here in my head." Shane pointed to his forehead.

"But they have enough to put an imitation out there that will question the integrity of Ecstasy."

"I admit it's a blow," Kayla replied, jumping in as the voice of reason, "but it's not the end of the world. Many of the top designers have had their fragrances imitated. It doesn't mean that Ecstasy will fail. We just have to make sure that we deliver the best product and the best campaign."

"Since when did you become the optimist?" Shane asked, glancing at her sideways. He'd never known Kayla to be this way.

"Since the both of you started acting like Neanderthals."

Ethan smiled. Only Kayla could put him in his place with a quick lash of her tongue. "I just don't like having our plans thwarted," he said, softening his voice.

Kayla gave him a look that said *much better.* "We have to find out who is behind the leak and this theft."

"I couldn't agree with you more," Shane said.

"I know you're going to hate to hear this, but we need to look at every employee in the lab," Kayla replied, "including Gabrielle."

Shane shook his head. "Gabby would never steal from us. She has the highest degree of integrity I've ever seen.

She would never do this." Even though they weren't speaking at the moment, Shane felt as if he knew Gabrielle well enough to know she wouldn't steal his hard work. *She wouldn't seduce him to get close to him, would she?*

Kayla noticed how adamant Shane was that Gabrielle couldn't possibly be the culprit, which could only mean that her brother was falling for Gabrielle. Kayla recognized the symptoms because he had the same look of denial she'd had about Ethan last year when she'd found herself falling in love with the man who'd taken over her family's company.

"Shane, you have to consider it. She *is* the newest employee to the lab," Kayla pressed the point.

"You don't know Gabby like I do."

Ethan noticed the intent look passing between both siblings as Shane spoke. He wondered if more was going on between the two chemists than he knew about. If there was, and Kayla knew, she would never tell him and break her brother's confidence. And he would never ask her to. "I agree with Kayla, Shane. We have to consider all possible suspects." He reached across the table and pressed his intercom. "Myra, can you please contact the head of security and have him come up here immediately?"

"Will do, Mr. Graham," a female voice said through the phone.

Gabrielle's stomach was a mass of nerves. Shane had never spoken to her that way, not even when he'd been angry with her when she'd first started at Adams Cosmetics. She couldn't believe he'd ordered her out of his office. He'd slammed his door and then minutes later come bursting through it and, without a word to anyone in the lab, had stormed out.

Did this have anything to do with the design leak to

the press? Should she have told him before now what was going on with her family and Andrew Jackson? Would he have believed her if she had?

When Shane returned to the lab, his expression was masked. Gabrielle knew something was amiss, but what? She decided she'd wait to approach him until they were alone. That moment didn't come until the end of day, because Shane dropped a bombshell that had the entire lab rattled.

"Everyone, gather around," Shane said, motioning for all the chemists to come forward in a circle.

"Is something wrong?" one of the other chemists asked.

Shane nodded. "It has come to my attention that someone accessed my safe without my permission."

"What does that mean?" Gabrielle asked.

"Ecstasy has been compromised," Shane replied. "Someone has the formula."

"Ohmigod, Shane!" Gabrielle's hand flew to her mouth. *How could something like this have happened with the high level of security at AC?* You had to have an access badge to get anywhere near the lab, and the process to get a badge included a background check and fingerprinting.

"It's not good," Shane said, "but at least they don't have all the notes."

Gabrielle wasn't buying Shane's positive spin. She knew this was a catastrophe. "But a good chemist could get darn close."

"They can imitate Ecstasy, but our product will be superior in quality and packaging."

"The bottle design has already been leaked to the press." One of the chemists, an Asian woman who typically was very shy, spoke up. "What's next?"

Shane rolled his eyes upward. "Does anyone want to

offer anything positive? Because trust me, the executive board and I have thought about every worst-case scenario."

"What's going to happen now?" Gabrielle inquired.

"An investigation will take place."

"Meaning that all of us are under suspicion?" the Asian woman spoke up again.

Gabrielle glanced up at Shane and knew the woman had hit the nail on the head. Every chemist in the lab would be under suspicion as the possible culprit, even though they'd each signed a nondisclosure agreement when they were hired.

"Shane, I've worked for this company for five years," the woman pressed. "You know me. You know I would never do this."

"Mai-Li," Shane said as he walked toward her and touched her shoulder. "I know you. I know all of you." He turned and faced his staff. "And I know you will all be cleared. But we must find who did this."

"We're here for you, Shane, whatever you need." Gabrielle offered a hesitant smile.

Shane turned, and this time he dazzled her with one of his trademark smiles. As always, Gabrielle's stomach did a somersault. "Thank you, I appreciate that."

Gabrielle waited for everyone to leave before she knocked on Shane's door. She poked her head inside. "Is it safe to enter?"

Shane lowered his head. "I'm so sorry, Gabby." He felt terrible. "I didn't mean to yell at you earlier. I was just really stressed. C'mon in." He motioned for her to enter.

"Do you have any idea who could have done this?" Gabrielle asked, sitting down.

"No." Shane shook his head, rose from his chair and

came and sat on the edge of the desk. "But it has to be someone with high-level access."

"Someone obviously has it out for your family."

"And there's only one person I know who hates my family enough to want to sabotage us, and that's Andrew Jackson."

"He's the owner of Jax Cosmetics, right?" Gabrielle asked. She'd decided to play it safe. Although she didn't have confirmation, she suspected Andrew was behind her father coming to her apartment with a sudden change of heart only to steal a photo of the prototype.

"Yes. He's my father's archrival and has been since the day my father stole my mother from Andrew."

Gabrielle's eyes grew large. She'd never heard this story before. "What happened?"

"Andrew and my father were friends and business partners. My father was poor, but Andrew was from a wealthy family, as was my mother. Back in the day, Andrew and my father talked about starting a cosmetics company together, but Andrew had a wandering eye, and my mother got fed up with Andrew's philandering ways and broke it off. She ended up marrying my father, much to Andrew's and her family's consternation. They disinherited her for many years."

"But didn't your father used to work at Graham International?"

"Yes, he had to," Shane answered. "He didn't have the capital to start his own business. So he toiled under Carter Graham, Ethan's father, for many years until he could save enough money to start Adams Cosmetics on his own. Needless to say, Carter felt betrayed when he left. All the time he'd spent cultivating my dad was lost, so there was a lot of animosity. Eventually, my grandmother forgave my mother and reinherited her and put money in trust for us, but by then Adams Cosmetics was a success. That's when Andrew started Jax Cosmetics as a rival company, just to rattle my father."

"That's an amazing story," Gabrielle said. "No wonder your family fought so hard to keep AC away from Ethan."

"My father was no saint," Shane replied. He respected his father a great deal, but he didn't have false illusions. Byron Adams had his faults. "He made a few bad decisions near the end and we had no choice but to merge with Graham International to avoid going under."

"So it all came full circle, back to GI," Gabrielle replied.

"And sometimes Ethan never lets us forget that he saved our hides," Shane replied. "And I have to admit, I resent his interference. But Kayla loves him, so I keep my mouth shut. It's just when he mouths off about my failures in the lab, it really gets my goat."

Gabrielle couldn't believe how much Shane was confiding in her. It was the first time he was allowing her a glimpse into his head. For the longest time, he'd given her surface information. *Perhaps she'd misread the situation and he did truly care for her?*

Nervously, Gabrielle wrung her hands. She really needed to talk to Shane about their relationship and her father, but after hearing his story, the timing wasn't right. She desperately wanted to get back to how they were in Paris. "I was thinking…that perhaps we could spend some time together this weekend…" Gabrielle's voice trailed off.

Shane looked at Gabby. Although he didn't know why she'd pushed him away several nights ago, he was happy to see that she'd had a change of heart. He had missed her. "I would love that, but I have some family commitments this weekend."

Gabrielle's mouth formed an O. She'd hoped they could

have some alone time and she could finally tell him the huge secret she'd been keeping from him about her father stealing the design.

"But…" Shane's mind started racing. "You could come with me. It's Kayla's baby shower, and instead of it being just the girls, it's going to be unisex. Ethan claimed that he's having the baby too and wants to open gifts." Shane could understand that. Carter Graham had been a cold son of a gun, and Ethan seemed determined to be a different kind of father. He'd only missed the one Lamaze class that Shane had subbed in for.

"I don't know." Gabrielle rose from her chair and paced his office. "Sounds like a family event and…"

"Listen." Shane jumped out of his chair and came over to stand beside her. "Courtney and Kayla already know we're dating, so why not tell my parents and Ethan?" He shrugged. "Who cares? We're adults, right?"

"Right." Gabrielle smiled back.

"Then I will pick you up tomorrow morning, bright and early. The baby shower is at 2:00 p.m., and that'll give us plenty of time to ride up and get unpacked and freshen up."

"Where are we going?" Gabrielle inquired. She'd assumed they'd be at the Adams family estate.

"Oh, you'll see," Shane said. "My family doesn't know how to do anything small."

Chapter 12

Shane picked Gabrielle up at 9:00 a.m. and, without telling her where they were going, headed toward Interstate 85. The conversation in the car was still somewhat strained, but she hoped to rectify that once they were alone, which would hopefully be sometime in the evening.

Gabrielle was shocked when less than an hour later they drove through the gates of Château Élan and arrived at the sixteenth-century-inspired inn. A bellboy greeted her and helped her out of the car. As she stepped out, Gabrielle was treated to a panoramic view of the north Georgia foothills, well-manicured lawns and surrounding vineyard. Shane wasn't lying when he'd said that his family didn't know how to celebrate small.

"This is where the baby shower is?" Gabrielle asked as the bellboy removed their overnight bags from Shane's trunk.

"Oh, Kayla had nothing to do with this spectacle,"

Shane said, walking around the car. "This was all Mother. You know, this is her first grandchild and all. She wanted it to be grand."

"That it is," Gabrielle said as they walked inside the chateau.

The inside was bright and airy with lots of sunlight from the skylights overhead, white columns and marble floors. Tons of planters sprinkled throughout the lobby held various plant species.

Once checked in, they went to their suite, which had a lush king-size bed. It was modern, yet simply decorated. Gabrielle peeked in the bathroom and found it held a bathtub for two. Memories of her and Shane in the marble tub in Paris came to mind, and Gabrielle warmed all over.

"Is everything to your liking, ma'am?" Shane came behind her and circled his arms around her waist.

"Of course." Gabrielle turned around in his arms. "Are you sure it's okay for me to be here?" She gave a nervous sweep of her tongue over her suddenly dry lips.

Shane caught that nervous moment and it made him want a taste. "Absolutely!" he stated fiercely. Hungrily. He crushed his lips against hers and parted them to deepen the kiss. His tongue surged inside Gabby's mouth, tasting every sweet cavern. He pulled her tightly against him, eager to feel those slender curves pressed against him. It had been too long.

Gabrielle felt his passion. Shane was kissing her as if she was the drink he'd been thirsting for all day. "Easy, boy." She pushed her hands against Shane's chest. "We do have a baby shower to get to in a couple of hours and…"

"If we get started, we won't want to stop?" Shane offered as he released her.

Gabrielle smiled. "Exactly!" She walked back into the bedroom.

"You promise to make it up to me later?" Shane asked. Gabrielle gave him a wink. "You better believe it."

Shane walked hand in hand with Gabrielle into one of the immaculately decorated ballrooms. He had to hand it to his mother. She knew her stuff. The room was done in white and blue since Kayla was having a boy. His mother had thought of every detail, from the white drapes hanging from the ceiling, to the linens on the table, to the blue fabric across the chairs—even the gift boxes for each guest had a blue ribbons around them.

Shane noticed some of the surprised faces on his family members as they walked over. Courtney and Kayla were not as surprised, but Ethan and his parents were clearly floored.

"Dad, Mom." Shane motioned Gabrielle forward. "I'd like you to meet Gabrielle Burton."

Although his mother was temporarily taken aback, she recovered with her usual aplomb and gave Gabrielle a hug and a kiss on the cheek. "Welcome, dear. We've heard nothing but the best things about you."

"Thank you, Mrs. Adams." Gabrielle smiled. "And Kayla," she said as she turned to Shane's sister, "you're looking as radiant as ever."

Kayla chuckled. "I look like a big whale, but thank you for saying so. How was the drive over?"

"We made it in good time," Shane said.

While Shane and Kayla talked, Courtney immediately zeroed in on Gabrielle. "Why didn't you tell me you were coming?" she whispered.

"Because I had no idea I was. It was a last-minute thing."

"You know this is big," Courtney replied. "Shane *never* introduces us to his women."

Gabrielle took that as a good sign until Ethan came over. "So you and Shane, huh?" he asked. "Why am I the last to know?" He'd watched his wife with Shane, and clearly she'd known about the relationship, because her mouth hadn't dropped open when they'd arrived.

"Mr. Graham…" Gabrielle began, but Ethan held up his hands.

"You owe me no explanation," he replied. "Who am I to judge? Kayla and I fell in love under the most unusual circumstances."

"Shane and I aren't in love," Gabrielle responded.

"Are you sure about that?" Ethan said, tilting his head in Shane's direction, who at the moment was staring intently at the two of them.

"Wow! You sure do like to surprise your mama," Elizabeth Adams commented to her son as the guests began arriving. Gabrielle had already been recruited by Courtney to help direct guests to their seats. "Why haven't you told me about Gabrielle before now?"

"There wasn't much to tell," Shane answered honestly. He watched as Gabrielle attended to one of the children who had wandered away. She was squatting down to the little girl's level and laughing with her. "We've been seeing each other for a while, and I guess you could say things heated up between us in Paris."

"And…?" She wasn't going to let Shane give her a pat answer.

"And I've come to care a great deal about Gabby."

"Enough to settle down?"

Shane glanced sideways at her. "Whoa there, Mom. Who said anything about settling down? Gabby and I are just enjoying each other. You should be happy you have a new grandbaby on the way to love and spoil."

"And of course I'm happy about that, Shane, but I want love for you, too. I can only hope that you find the kind of lasting love your father and I have had over these last forty years."

"I don't know," Shane said. "What you and Dad have is pretty rare."

"But not impossible to find," his mother replied, "if you're willing to let love in."

Shane thought about what his mother said as the baby shower got under way. He and Gabrielle, his parents and Courtney sat at one table, while Ethan and Kayla sat center stage with small circular tables around them. Family, friends and many of their work colleagues had driven up to Château Élan to celebrate with them. It showed Shane just how well liked they were by those who worked for them, which is why he was finding it hard to believe that any of his chemists or anyone else at AC could have stolen from them. The questions were driving him crazy, but Shane refused to let them spoil the day. He reached across the table and squeezed Gabrielle's hand, and she smiled back at him. When he glanced up, he noticed Courtney watching him.

Surprisingly, the shower turned out to be fun, with both men and women contributing in the games. Not to mention, the loot of gifts that Ethan and Kayla collected for their son. When it was all over, it was nearly dinnertime.

The party continued as their mother had arranged for a private family dinner at Le Clos, an intimate restaurant inside the winery. They savored the three-course menu prepared with local organic ingredients and everyone, except Kayla, tasted some of the finest wines the winery had to offer.

"You realize this bites," Kayla commented. "You know I'm pregnant, and you know I love wine, and you have my baby shower at a winery? It's cruel and unusual punishment."

They all laughed and continued to talk throughout the evening. After dessert, they shared coffee and cappuccinos before Kayla and Ethan eventually retired to the Governor's Suite for the evening.

"Poor thing looks pooped," Courtney commented.

"Well, she is due in a few weeks," her mother replied.

Shane faked a yawn himself and stretched out his arms. "Hmm… I'm pooped, too. I think we're going to head off to bed." He scooted his chair out and helped Gabrielle out of hers.

She noticed the looks of disbelief on Courtney's and his father's faces, and she blushed several shades. "Thank you for a lovely evening, Mr. and Mrs. Adams." She inclined her head to Shane's parents. "Courtney, good to see you as always."

"You get some *rest* now," Courtney said.

Gabrielle couldn't help but notice the humor in her voice.

Once they were back in their suite, Shane and Gabrielle were as hungry for each other as they had been earlier that day. They tore at each other's clothes as if they were a barrier. They'd gone nearly a week without making love, and Gabrielle thought she was going to explode. Her nipples were swollen and aching with desire that only Shane could quench. They kissed with lips, teeth and tongue, both lost in the pleasure.

When they were both naked and their clothes were in a pile on the floor, they met together on the bed. The softness of Gabrielle's curves molded perfectly with the hardness of Shane's body. He nudged her backward until she fell back against the pillows. He pushed her legs apart and ground his arousal against her tempting heat.

Gabrielle felt the thick length of his shaft pressing against her, and she circled her legs around his trim waist, easily allowing him entrance. Shane had a wild gleam in his eyes, and she could tell that he wanted this as much as she did. He slid inside her and filled her completely.

Pure pleasure coursed through Shane as Gabrielle moved herself up and down his shaft. Shane loved being inside Gabby and having her silken heat tight around him. He thrust hard and fast inside her, and Gabby met each thrust by rocking her hips and meeting his rhythm. Soon they were on a frantic ride to completion, one that neither of them wanted to end. Gabrielle climaxed first, but it didn't take Shane long to give out an exultant shout of ecstasy that sent him spiraling back down to earth.

As they lay in bed the next morning, Shane thought about how he didn't want to go back to Atlanta. He and Gabby had connected in the same way as they had in Paris. Their bodies had no trouble speaking to each other, so why was it so hard for their mouths to?

Shane brushed back several tendrils of hair from Gabby's forehead and looked down at her. *When had this fiery diva become so important to him, and why did he feel as if he might not be able to live without her?*

Gabrielle stirred underneath him and then glanced up at him with sleepy eyes. "Hey, you."

"Hey, yourself." Shane pressed his lips to her mouth.

"Don't tell me you're ready again?" Gabrielle said. They'd made love twice last night.

Shane laughed. "No. Even he needs to rest," he said, looking down at his member. "So why don't you tell me what's on your mind? I feel like there's something you're keeping from me."

He was right. She wanted to talk to him about her father

and the stolen design, Andrew Jackson and the entire mess, but it didn't seem like the right time. She chose instead to talk about her other least favorite topic, their relationship.

"I know there's something, Gabby. Whatever it is, just tell me."

Gabrielle scooted toward the pillows until she was in the crook of Shane's arm. "I guess I don't know whether we should still keep going."

"Are you tired of me already?" Shane asked, jokingly. He couldn't believe they were having this conversation after the night they'd just shared.

"Of course not, but we both know this isn't going to last, so maybe we should get out now before anyone gets hurt."

"So you think I'll hurt you?"

Gabrielle looked down "Not intentionally…"

"Gabby, I think the world of you. I love your smile, your warmth, your passion for what you do."

"What does that mean?"

"I don't know," Shane answered honestly. "I'm figuring it out."

Should she wait for Shane to decide whether he was in love with her? Because right now, at this moment, Gabrielle knew beyond a shadow of a doubt that she was in love with Shane. It had been gradual, but there was no mistaking it. She loved him. "I don't know…." She shook her head. "There's just so much going on…." She looked at Shane, wanting to tell him the truth about her parents and Andrew Jackson, but she felt guilty.

A sinking feeling formed in Shane's stomach, and he began thinking the worst. "Gabby, is there something more you want to tell me?" He couldn't read her expression or tell what she was thinking, and it scared him. Usually she was an open book, heart on her sleeve.

"No." Gabrielle retreated farther away on the bed. "You know, we should really get going. I have a few things to take care of today." She jumped out of the bed and headed to the bathroom.

Shane heard the shower seconds later and guessed that meant it was indeed time to go home. He didn't know what had just happened, but obviously Gabrielle was struggling with something that she couldn't share with him.

The drive back to Atlanta was fraught with tension. Neither Shane nor Gabrielle said much, and the few times they did speak revolved around the weather or traffic on the interstate.

Gabrielle felt terrible for jumping up the way she had at the chateau, but when she'd looked in Shane's eyes, she couldn't find the right words to tell him how she'd been duped by her own family. Even worse, she felt that he would blame her for the leak. It was her negligence that could cost his family millions.

Shane was frustrated by the seesaw that was his relationship with Gabrielle. One moment they were up, enjoying a great weekend with his family and making love, the next moment she was shutting him out and running away from him. She couldn't get out of the car fast enough yesterday when he'd brought her back to her apartment.

It was Monday, and now he had the unfortunate task of listening in as security interrogated every member of his staff. Gabrielle was next. Ethan had brought in a top-notch investigator who was skilled at getting to the truth. He'd even brought in a lie-detector test, which he would offer to each chemist. He'd already put two of his chemists through the wringer, quizzing them about their background, their education, their work history, until Mai-Li had finally rushed out of the room weeping. Shane was furious, as he thought it was over the top, but this time Kayla had stood by her husband.

"We need to get to the truth, Shane," Kayla said when he'd asked her to halt the proceeding.

It made Shane sick to his stomach to treat his people this way. He was happy when the lobby receptionist informed him a package had been couriered over to him. Shane left the remaining chemists, including Gabby, sitting in the hall to head to the lobby.

He accepted the package and didn't waste any time ripping open the envelope. Shane stopped dead in his tracks when he saw the contents of the package. Inside was a picture of Gabby and Andrew Jackson at a restaurant. Shane immediately slid the picture back inside the envelope and glanced around to make sure no one else had seen it. He quickly walked back to reception.

"*Who* delivered this package?" Shane inquired, holding up the envelope.

"A courier service," the woman answered. "Is something wrong, Mr. Adams?"

"Uh, no." Shane gave her a kind smile. "I'm sorry if I sounded angry. It wasn't directed at you." And with that, he stormed off in the direction of the elevators. What the hell was going on? Why had Gabrielle had a meeting with Andrew Jackson? Was he trying to recruit her? Or worse yet, did Gabby have something to do with the leak of the design or the missing formula? *Was she in cahoots this whole time with Jackson?* Had he been duped?

Shane's hands were shaking as he pressed the down button to go back to the laboratory. His first inclination was to confront Gabrielle with the incriminating evidence, but he didn't have any real proof that she was involved in the theft. So, he went back to the scene of one of the crimes. He was surprised to find the laboratory locked. Mai-Li clearly hadn't returned after her meltdown, and the other chemists must have gone to lunch. Shane glanced down at his Swiss watch, which read 1:00 p.m.

It was perfect timing. Shane knew what he had to do, but he didn't relish going through Gabrielle's desk or her belongings. He used his master key to open her desk and rifled through several papers. He found nothing at first, but then he pulled out the drawers entirely. It was then that he came across the most damning evidence of all. When he turned over one of the desk drawers, tucked inside was a copy of the formula to Ecstasy.

All the air in the room whooshed out of Shane's lungs, and he took a step backward, falling against the lab counter. There was no reason for Gabrielle to have the formula and certainly not hidden in her desk. She had to be working *with* or *for* Andrew Jackson. She'd obviously insinuated herself into the laboratory so she could spy on Adams Cosmetics and report back to Andrew Jackson. And Andrew, being the slimy bastard he was, was ratting her out by sending that photograph of their secret meeting.

Gabrielle had used him. She'd played the sweet, innocent chemist in need of a makeover, and they'd all bought it. Kayla and Ethan had been taken in by her credentials, and Courtney had fallen for the ugly-duckling act. And he, well, he'd been had. Worst of all, Gabrielle had acted as if she didn't want him at first, but it had all been a ploy. She'd intentionally played hard to get to make him fall for her. And he had, hook, line and sinker.

Shane turned away and allowed his head to fall into his hands. Gabrielle Burton had set him and the entire Adams family up. *How could he have been so blind? How could he have allowed himself to be taken in by her?* He'd even begun to think that perhaps his mom was right, and he should try the long-term-commitment thing. Gabby had been so good at fooling him that he'd actually believed she had sincere feelings for him.

Although Gabby had made a fool of him, Shane wasn't going to let her get away with it. He would make her pay.

Gabrielle was tired of the endless questions the investigator kept asking her. No matter how many ways he tried to rephrase them, her story was the same. She had nothing to hide, until he asked her why she'd stayed in Paris so long after school. That's when she faltered.

"Why is that any of your business?" Gabrielle inquired.

"I'm just trying to get to the truth here, Ms. Burton," the investigator returned.

"And the truth of the matter is that my reasons for staying abroad were personal and do not concern my employ at Adams Cosmetics." There was no way Gabrielle was about to get into her relationship with her parents.

Just then, Shane came walking through the door. "The interview is over," he told the investigator.

"Mr. Adams," he began, but Shane cut him off.

"I said the interview is over," Shane barked and then glared at Gabrielle.

Gabrielle didn't know why Shane was furious, but she was grateful that he'd stopped the interview when he did.

"Why don't you wait outside." Shane kept the conference door open. "I'll call you when I'm done." Reluctantly, the investigator headed toward the exit and Shane closed the door.

"Oh, thank God." Gabrielle rose from her chair and came toward Shane with her arms open. "That guy was giving me the creeps." She gave Shane a hug, but noticed he didn't return it. She stepped away and looked at Shane. His eyes were cold with contempt, and it scared her. "What's wrong?"

"The jig is up, Gabrielle."

Gabrielle noted how he didn't call her Gabby as he usually did. That didn't bode well. "I don't understand."

Shane threw down the photograph of her and Andrew Jackson for her to see. "You want to explain that?" he asked, looking like a volcano on the verge of erupting.

Gabrielle picked up the photo, and when she saw what it was, a soft gasp escaped her lips. *No, not now.* Her mind raced. *Please, God, not now.* She'd wanted to tell him herself at the chateau, but she had chickened out. And now here it was in color. There was no denying she knew Andrew Jackson. *How could she explain?* She would have to try. Her life depended on it. "Shane…"

"Don't even bother to lie," Shane replied. "A picture is worth a thousand words."

"I wasn't about to lie."

"Weren't you?" He raised a brow. "Like when you acted like you didn't know who Andrew Jackson was? When in fact, you'd been meeting with him secretly?"

"I know this picture looks damning," she responded. Her hands shook as she held the evidence. "I wanted to tell you about it. I even tried to at the chateau."

"But you just couldn't find the words?" Shane taunted. "What do you take me for, Gabrielle?"

She flinched at the harsh sound in his voice. "There is an explanation for that photo, if you care to hear it."

Shane laughed bitterly. "If I care to hear it? Are you kidding me? You have been playing me and my family for fools since the day you got here from Paris. Is that when Andrew recruited you? Or was it after that you decided to turn on us?"

"Neither!"

"And you expect me to believe that?"

The distrust in Shane's eyes chilled Gabrielle to her core. She gulped hard as hot tears began slipping down her cheeks. "Shane, please… I know this looks bad, but you have to believe I would never hurt you or your family." After everything they'd shared, he at least had to believe that she wasn't capable of such deception.

"Crocodile tears. Wow!" His voice was bitter. "Even now, you can turn them on at will, and I almost want to believe you." He held up his finger. "Almost, but not anymore, Gabrielle. You may have played me for a sucker, but no more. You gave Andrew a photograph of the prototype and my formula, and that photo is proof."

Gabrielle shook her head. "I… I didn't do it, Shane." She tried to take in slow, shallow breaths so she could calm down and try to convince him, but she couldn't get any air into her lungs. "I…I swear it."

"I don't believe you," Shane replied. "Matter of fact, I don't want to hear anything that comes out of your lying mouth. We're over, Gabrielle."

Gabrielle stared wordlessly at him, her heart pounding in her chest. *Shane didn't believe her.* He truly thought she'd faked every moment they'd ever shared together. And it broke her heart. Stunned, she rushed out of the room.

Chapter 13

"No, you're wrong!" Courtney shook her head adamantly later that evening. Shane had called a family meeting in the living room at the Adams estate. "I know Gabby, and she would never do what you're accusing her of."

"I wouldn't have thought it either, Courtney," Shane said. "Don't you think *I* of all people wanted to believe it wasn't true? But the evidence is right there." He pointed to the photograph of Gabrielle and Andrew Jackson lying on the cocktail table and the copy of the formula. "That's hard to refute."

"Well, did you give her a chance to explain?" Courtney asked. She could just see Shane going after her with guns blazing, especially if he thought he'd been fooled. She knew Shane was starting to fall in love with Gabby, so it must have hurt seeing such incendiary evidence. Which meant he'd shown her no mercy.

"What's there to explain, Courtney?" their father said.

"It's right there. She's been conspiring with that bastard Jackson this entire time, cozying up to *my son* and *my daughter* to get in our inner circle. Sounds exactly like Jackson to me."

"I'm with Courtney on this," their mother replied. "I saw Gabby with you, Shane, and I just can't believe that this young woman would be that devious. She was crazy about you. It was written all over her face."

Shane turned away. *That's what he'd thought, too, but he'd been wrong.* He'd been completely taken in by her go-get-'em persona at work; her modest, yet naive look; and her passionate nature in the bedroom. "She was a good actress."

Courtney rushed over to Shane and spun him around to look at her. "You can't believe this, Shane. Tell me you don't really believe this."

"Courtney, you're much too close to this to see the truth," Ethan said, taking a much-needed sip of Scotch. Even he'd been thrown by this latest development. He'd always thought himself to be a good judge of character, and he'd had such a good feeling about Gabrielle. Apparently, he'd been wrong, as had Shane.

"What do you know?" Courtney sniped at her brother-in-law.

"Easy, Courtney," Kayla said. She attempted to rise from the sofa, but given her enormous belly, she couldn't muster it. Ethan leaned over to help his wife up. "If you'll excuse me, I need a potty break. You guys are making me nervous."

Kayla left the room, but that didn't stop the bickering. Courtney was more determined than ever to stick up for Gabrielle's good name.

"What I know," Ethan replied, "is that I could bring a

lawsuit against her and Andrew Jackson for corporate espionage and stealing intellectual property."

"Serves them both right," Byron huffed. "Andrew just
can't stand to see us succeed. He'll do anything to sabotage us. I should go over there right now and give him a
piece of my mind." Byron made as if he was heading for
the door, but his wife's voice stopped him.

"And what would that accomplish, Byron? It would just
put you in jail for assault. Because you know Andrew
would press charges."

Byron paused midstep and turned back around. "I sup-
pose you have a point, Elizabeth."

"She does," Ethan concurred. "The last thing we need
is bad press. We already have a fragrance in jeopardy."

"What are you going to do about all this, Ethan?" Byron
asked.

Ethan smiled that his father-in-law was finally manag-
ing to call him by his first name. "Publicity is using the
leak to generate press, and no one knows that the formula
has been stolen. I made sure of it."

"We're moving up the date of the launch," Kayla said,
waddling back into the room. She was exhausted and
ready for the baby to come.

"I, for one, can't wait," Shane said after being quiet for
some time. "Getting this one to the finish line has been
mentally exhausting."

"And what about Gabby?" Courtney asked Shane.
"Don't you care about her anymore?"

Shane replied without hesitation. "I never want to see
Gabrielle Burton again. And I want her to stay as far away
from me and my family as possible."

The drive to Marietta, along with a week of unemploy-
ment, gave Gabrielle plenty of time to reflect on what she

had to do. She'd avoided doing this because she'd hoped that her parents would have the courage to face her, but since they were both acting like cowards, she would have to confront them.

She knew her parents' Sunday routine and, as expected, found their car in the driveway. She'd timed it perfectly. Clearly much hadn't changed in all these years.

Gabrielle used the front-door key she'd kept with her out of nostalgia and found that it still worked. Her parents were seated in the parlor having a cup of tea and biscuits after church, as they'd done every Sunday for as long as she remembered.

"Mama, Daddy," she said from the doorway.

Startled, her mother dropped her teacup and it crashed into tiny pieces on the floor. Her mother rose to clean it up, but Gabrielle stood in her path. "Leave it! You're not going anywhere."

"Excuse me, young lady?" Her mother's eyes were wide with indignation.

"I said sit down," Gabrielle repeated. She glanced over at her father, who was doing his best to be invisible and silently looking down at the floor. It wasn't working.

Reluctantly, her mother sat back down in her chair. "What are you doing here, Gabby?"

"He knows exactly why I'm here." Gabrielle pointed to her father.

"What did you do, James?" Her mother looked at him questioningly.

"Don't act like you don't know, Mama." Gabrielle sighed. "It's why you haven't returned my calls."

"I didn't return your calls because your father said you'd had enough and wanted no part of us," her mother responded. "Ever."

Gabrielle nodded. So her father was even lying to her

mother. Figures. She folded her arms across her chest. "I came here to say my piece and then I am leaving, for good this time. And I'm not *ever* coming back."

"Gabby, don't be overly dramatic," her mother said.

"You don't get to dismiss me like I'm unimportant, like you have for all these years," Gabrielle snapped back.

Her father shifted in his chair but still remained silent.

"You have nothing to say, huh?" Gabrielle asked, coming from behind him and crouching down to look him in the face. She dropped her purse to the floor. "Not after you rifled through my briefcase and took photos of my company's prototype, so you could sell it to Andrew Jackson? Why don't you have the courage to admit what you did?"

"James!" Her mother sounded genuinely shocked, as if she hadn't known what her father had done.

"Oh, yes." Gabrielle rose so she could face them both. "Daddy came to my apartment like he wanted to reconcile with me and finally have a father-daughter relationship, even hugged me for the first time in twelve years to seal the deal. Hmm… Now wasn't that a little over the top?" Gabrielle laughed bitterly. "You stole from your own daughter, for what?"

"I needed the money," her father finally spoke. "And in return, Andrew agreed to pay off my gambling debts."

"Gambling?" her mother asked. "Since when?"

"Apparently for some time," Gabrielle answered. "So much so that Andrew Jackson came and asked me to spy at Adams Cosmetics, and when I refused, he sent Daddy to do his dirty work. And if that wasn't good enough, Andrew snapped a photo of us together so it would appear like I'd been working with him all along. Brilliant, huh!"

"I… I had no idea about that," her father replied nervously. "Andrew never mentioned a thing."

"Well, you don't have to worry now, do you, because your debt has been paid. While I, on the other hand, have been fired and will probably be blacklisted at every reputable cosmetics company! So I'll have nothing. Are you happy, Daddy? Are you happy that finally I have nothing?"

"Of course not," he said.

When Gabrielle looked over at her mother, she was crying in her handkerchief.

"What are you crying for?" Gabrielle hissed. Everything she'd been bottling up for the past fifteen years came tumbling out like a tsunami. "You've never cared about me, the one child you have left since Seth died."

"Don't you speak his name," her mother cried. "Don't you dare!"

"I have every right to speak his name. He wasn't just your son. He was *my brother!* And I lost him, too, but you two—" she pointed to her parents "—couldn't see through your own grief to comfort *me.* You forgot I existed. I might as well have died out there in that ocean with Seth!"

"Why are you saying such hurtful things," her mother cried. "It would have killed us losing you both."

"I'm saying it because it's true. You fed and clothed me, but you forgot to *love me.*"

Silence ensued for several moments before her father finally said. "We have always loved you."

"Always," her mother cried, but her words sounded hollow.

"You've never shown it." Now Gabrielle was crying, too, even though she'd vowed she would hold it together. She didn't want to let them see that they'd broken her, but they had. She'd finally snapped, and she had nothing left to lose. "Up until last month, you hadn't hugged me in fifteen years. And I was so desperate for your love and happy that you were ready to start anew and be a father again, that I didn't see you were just using me to get out of debt."

"I'm sorry, Gabrielle." Her father hung his head low. "I should never have done it. I was just so desperate. But things are better now. I'm going to AA and Gamblers Anonymous, and they are helping me work through my issues."

Gabrielle laughed bitterly. "I'm so glad you can move on, Daddy. Because I've been stuck here, stuck here in the past, unable to move forward, because I've been waiting for the moment when you guys would love me again, like you did when Seth was alive. But no more." Gabrielle shook her head. "You are not worthy of my love, neither of you." She bent to pick up her purse. "That's why from this point forward, I consider myself an orphan. I have no parents." She rushed toward the door.

"Gabby, no!" Her mother jumped up and grabbed her arm to stop her. "Please don't leave. We can't lose you now."

Gabrielle shook her head. "You lost me a long time ago." And with a clear conscience, she walked away from her parents forever.

Her next stop was Shane's apartment. She didn't relish going over there to pick up her things, but there was no way around it. She was going to have to face him one last time.

Shane wasn't home, but the doorman was kind enough to let her in. Gabrielle began to pack up the few things she'd left at his place: a jogging suit, slippers, lingerie, toothbrush and hair dryer. She was just bringing a few odd toiletries back to the bedroom to finish packing her gym bag when she heard the front door slam.

Fear knotted inside her and Gabrielle prepared herself to face Shane. He'd had some time to think it over, and she hoped he wasn't as angry with her as he had been several days before. But when she saw him, she knew it was worse.

Shane's eyes were cold and aloof as they surveyed her pushing the toiletries in her bag. His vexation at seeing her was evident, but he didn't yell. Instead he walked out of the bedroom and back into the living room. If he had screamed at her, it would have been better, because it would show that she still meant something to him. But this cold treatment meant he felt nothing for her.

She zipped up her bag and came into the living room. Shane was sitting on his supersize leather sofa looking straight ahead. The TV was directly in front of him, but it wasn't on. He was intent on ignoring her.

"Shane…" Gabrielle dropped her bag to the floor and walked toward him. She sat down on the ottoman in front of Shane, but when she reached for his hand, he retreated farther onto the couch.

He refused to look at her and she nervously bit her lip. A stab of guilt went through her because she could have prevented this if she'd been honest with him from the start. "I can't leave here with you believing the…the worst about me." Her voice broke as she continued. "I did not betray your family."

Still Shane said nothing.

"I would never hurt you or Courtney. Courtney has been like a little sister to me, and she's treated me with the utmost respect. And Kayla and Ethan have both been wonderful bosses. I couldn't ask to be part of a better family company than Adams Cosmetics."

It was then that Shane finally looked up at her. His eyes were cloudy with something she couldn't quite put her finger on. Disappointment? Disgust? Or was it regret that they wouldn't get the chance to explore the feelings they'd developed for one another?

When Shane continued to remain silent, Gabrielle decided to speak honestly. She tried to hold her tears in, but her eyes bordered with them. "Being around your family has reminded me of what I lost. I had a family once..." Tears blinded her eyes and choked her voice. "And I lost them when we lost Seth." She wiped away the tears with the back of her hand. "...And I never got them back. So being with you and your family made me feel like I belonged again, like I was part of a family. And that meant the world to me. I just can't leave here without you knowing that what we shared was real and special to me, and I'll never forget it."

A slight vestige of hope lay in Shane's eyes. Gabrielle reached out to stroke his cheek, and this time he didn't pull away. "*I* would never steal from you or your family. Please tell me you believe that."

Shane caught the inflection in her tone and finally spoke. "So you didn't do it, but you know who did?"

Her surprise that Shane had heard the inflection in her tone registered on her face, and she stared back tongue-tied.

"Well? I'm waiting for an answer." He looked at Gabby and the anguish he saw in her eyes made him want to believe every word she was saying. If she hadn't done it, then she knew who did. And the fact that she wasn't revealing who had sabotaged his family's company, that she was protecting them, hurt even more.

Despite everything that her father had done, Gabrielle didn't want him to be thrown in jail. When she continued to remain silent, Shane turned his head away. Slowly, Gabrielle rose from the couch and picked up her bag. "I'm sorry you think so little of me," she said, opening the door. Shane's back was still to her, but she decided to finally say how she truly felt. What did she have to lose? "But I *do* care for you, Shane. I think I always have, and I always will."

Shane heard a long pause. Had Gabrielle changed her mind? Was she going to stand and fight? Was she going to reveal who'd really done it? He quickly jumped up from the couch, but when he turned, he found the front door swinging open. He sunk down on the couch and clutched his head in his hands. Gabrielle, who'd been lying to him all along, was out of his life for good. So, why did it feel as if someone had just ripped his heart out of his chest?

Chapter 14

"I honestly can't believe the man's nerve," Kayla said when Shane came to her office. She'd just received her mail and was shocked to discover an invitation from Jax Cosmetics to attend its annual party that Friday. She'd immediately called down to the lab and Shane had rushed right up and found her on the couch. He'd thought she was going into labor, but she'd assured him she wasn't.

"Dad always said he had balls of steel," Shane commented, coming to sit beside her on the couch.

"Such language, Shane," Kayla chastised. "You are in the presence of a lady."

"Sorry, sis." He attempted a smile, even though he didn't feel like one. He hadn't felt much these days. He'd been walking through the haze that was his life for the past week. Even though he had the proof, it still hadn't sunken in that Gabrielle had betrayed him. And then there was that last comment of hers that *she* hadn't stole from them. It was clear that she knew who had, but she refused to give the person up. *She was protecting someone.* So why was he still trying to think the best of her? Gabrielle hadn't even tried to defend herself.

"How are you doing, anyway?" Kayla asked. "I know that photo must have come as quite a shock to you. I had never seen you that close with a woman before. And at Château Élan, if I hadn't known any better, I would have sworn you were in love with the woman."

"If I was or wasn't, it's inconsequential now," Shane said, "because what we had, or what I thought we had, is over. It was a lie."

"But your feelings weren't, Shane," Kayla said, grasping her brother's hand. "You always thought you weren't capable of real love, but you are. I saw it."

"And look where it got me," Shane said, "Looking like a fool. Love isn't worth this kind of heartache."

"So are you finally admitting it? That you love Gabrielle?"

"I admit nothing." Shane rose from the sofa. "Now that I know you're not in labor, I can go back to the lab."

"What did you tell your staff about Gabrielle?"

"I haven't yet," Shane said. He'd lied and told them she'd had an unexpected emergency and would be out for several days. "But I will, soon." He headed to the door.

"Wait! What are we going to do about this?" Kayla asked, holding up the invitation.

"We should go," he responded. Not only was he curious to see what Jax Cosmetics was up to, but he wanted to look that slimy Andrew Jackson in the face and tell him he may have won a round in the battle, but Adams Cosmetics would always win the war.

"Gabby, you don't have to do this," Courtney said when she arrived at Gabrielle's apartment midweek and found her friend packing.

"Yes, I do. I need to get away."

"What are you going to do?" Courtney asked, pacing the floor. "This is all so out of control. I really can't believe this is happening. I wish I could do something."

"This is not for you to fix, Courtney."

"I know, but I still feel bad. Where are you going now?"

"My friend Mariah is dating this flight attendant who gave me a free buddy ticket, so I'm going to fly back to Paris on Friday night and use the time to clear my head and figure out what my next step is."

Courtney turned up her nose. "You're going to fly standby?"

Gabrielle laughed because Courtney made it sound like a dirty word. "It'll save me money while I figure out what to do."

"Absolutely not!" Courtney said. "You'll use the family jet."

"Courtney!" Gabrielle sighed at her extravagance. "I couldn't possibly. Your family already thinks I've stolen from them, and now you want me to fly on the family jet? I can't."

"It's my jet, too," Courtney said with a pout. "And I should be able to say who can use it."

Gabrielle stopped packing and turned to her newfound friend. "I doubt your family would agree."

"Who cares what they think," Courtney said and grabbed both of Gabrielle's hands. "I care what *I* think, and I know you didn't do this."

Gabrielle smiled warmly. "How can you be so sure? You never even asked if I did it."

Courtney squeezed her hands. "I didn't have to. I know you didn't."

Gabrielle's eyes filled with tears. "Thank you for believing in me. I just wish Shane did."

"Shane is running scared," Courtney replied, "scared that you're the first woman to make him feel something. It's easier for him to think the worst, because then he'll be able to deny his feelings…which are that he's in love with you."

"You think so?" Gabrielle wasn't sure she could believe that. He may care for her, but love? That might be a stretch.

Courtney noted the hopeful sound in Gabrielle's voice. "I know so. I know my brother. Just like I know you. You're meant to be together."

"I wish I could believe that," Gabrielle said, "but I don't see how we can overcome this."

"Perhaps some time away will make my brother see the error of his ways, but if I were you, I would come back and fight for my man."

"Is that what you would do?"

"Hell, yes!"

The night of the Jax Cosmetics party, Shane felt a void, and it wasn't because someone in the family was missing. His father and mother were both waiting in the living room attired in their fancy duds—his dad in a tuxedo and his mother in a simple two-piece gown with a satin skirt. Kayla and Ethan had arrived a few moments before, and his sister, although nine months pregnant, looked radiantly beautiful in a one-shoulder chiffon gown that flowed out from her increasing bosom. Then of course, there was Courtney, Ms. Fashionista, in her four-inch high heels. She was stunningly glamorous in a lead-colored mesh gown with silver and gold sequins down the bodice. Everyone would certainly see his little sis from a million miles away with all that bling.

Deep down, Shane knew why he felt a void. It was because Gabby wasn't there with him. He'd been trying to banish her to the far recesses of his mind, but it wasn't working, even after a two-hour workout with his personal trainer. She was ingrained in his thoughts and in his memory. Everywhere he went he saw images of her in his mind.

"Shane, you okay?" Courtney asked, walking toward him with her hand on her hip. He was standing by the mantel looking dour.

"I'm fine," he said testily.

"Do you understand why we're going to this fiasco?" their mother asked, as she walked over and gently squeezed his arm. "Because I sure don't."

"We're going there to show Andrew Jackson that he can't keep us down and that we Adamses stick together," Kayla answered.

"And Grahams," Ethan added.

"Of course, baby." Kayla kissed her husband's cheek.

"Personally, I'd like to wipe the floor with Jackson," their father responded.

"There's not going to be raucousness tonight, Byron," his wife said. "Promise me."

"Oh, Elizabeth." Bryon waved his hand. "I'm just blowing a little smoke."

"You make sure that's all it is," his wife warned. She refused to have Byron make a spectacle of himself and their entire family. She wouldn't give Andrew that satisfaction. She knew why he'd invited the Adams family to his soiree—he wanted to rub their face in it. After all these years, she was amazed that Andrew could still hold a grudge. He'd married another woman and had a son named Jasper and a stepdaughter, Monica. Why was he still holding on to the past?

"I promise." Byron crossed his heart.

"Well, if that's all settled, are we ready to go?" Ethan asked.

"Let's roll," Shane said.

The Jax Cosmetics party was every bit as over the top and ostentatious as Andrew Jackson could make it. Shane was surprised that even with all the money Andrew must have spent on it, it lacked taste.

There were too many balloons, too many pictures of Andrew and too much press, including the tabloids. When they arrived, the red carpet was out, but they could barely move across it.

Waiting at the door in all of his six-foot-five glory was Andrew, his wife, Blythe, and stepdaughter, Monica. "Well, I'll be a monkey's uncle," Andrew said with a thick country accent. "If it isn't the Adams family and Ethan Graham."

"Oh, don't sound so shocked, Jackson," Byron replied when he came face-to-face with his nemesis. "You *did* invite us."

"Aw shucks, I guess I did," Andrew said and laughed.

"And we're so happy you could make it," Monica said, her voice dripping with sarcasm.

Shane wasn't surprised that Monica didn't want them there, because it meant there would be seven more people for Andrew to ignore her for. Monica Jackson was always living in someone else's shadow, and it was usually Jasper's shadow, Andrew's son with his first wife.

"Monica." Shane inclined his head toward the petite woman.

While every other woman was wearing an evening gown, Monica Jackson was wearing a tuxedo pantsuit, and although it was tailored perfectly, it made her seem masculine.

"Well, if it isn't wonder boy," Monica replied, looking Shane up and down. "Come up with any new creations lately?"

"Well, if I did, I'm sure Jax Cosmetics would be sniffing around ready to pick up the scraps," Shane responded and turned back around to his parents.

"It's a pleasure to see you, Elizabeth," Andrew said and reached for his mother's hand, but Byron stepped in the way. The two men locked gazes, neither one backing down.

Elizabeth grasped her husband's arm. "You as well, Andrew. Blythe." She acknowledged Andrew's second wife, who stood silent at his side thanks to her husband's larger-than-life personality. Blythe didn't respond and instead merely stared daggers at her. "Why don't we all go inside?"

"Good idea, Mom," Shane said and seconds later the family was moving into the foyer. What immediately caught Shane's attention was the big placard standing at the doorway of the entrance into the ballroom. He was the first to see it, as Ethan and Kayla were talking to several industry leaders and his parents were in what appeared to be a heated argument. Most likely about his father almost coming to blows with Andrew for attempting to touch his mother. A strange sense of foreboding came over Shane, and he knew the evening was not going to end well.

Shane stared at the placard of none other than Noelle Warner, an Academy Award–winning actress who also just so happened to be the ex-Adams Cosmetics spokeswoman. Clearly, Jax Cosmetics had snapped her up at the first opportunity to stick it to the Adams family, and Shane was sure Noelle had wholeheartedly agreed.

Last year, Ethan had hired his ex-girlfriend Noelle to replace Courtney as the AC spokesmodel, which had not sat well with the family. Noelle had seen it as a way back into Ethan's bed, because Ethan and Kayla's marriage had started out as one of convenience. But Noelle had miscalculated because Ethan and Kayla had fallen in love. And the fallout was that she'd nearly destroyed their marriage and almost cost them their unborn son when Kayla had fallen down a flight of stairs after an argument with Noelle.

Shane heard a sharp intake of breath from behind him and then he heard, "What the hell!"

"He ambushed us," Ethan hissed from behind Shane. "He brought us here knowing full well he'd hired that she devil after I fired her. Kayla, I'm so sorry." He turned to his wife with apologetic eyes.

"Of course he did," Shane replied, turning around. "Andrew likes nothing better than to stick it to us." He walked over to his sister's other side. "Kayla, don't let Andrew or Noelle get to you. They aren't worth it."

Shane watched Kayla take deep breaths in and out of her nose as the Lamaze coach had taught her. Clearly she wasn't happy about this latest turn of events, and he could see she was trying her best to keep calm.

Their parents must have seen Kayla in distress, because they quickly walked over. "What's wrong?" Byron asked, looking down at her.

"See for yourself." Shane pointed in the direction of the placard.

"That bastard!" Byron yelled. "Where is he?" He glanced around the lobby looking for Andrew Jackson.

"Byron," Elizabeth warned. "You promised me."

"That was before he upset our daughter!"

"And I think it's about to get worse," Shane said when he saw Noelle Warner come slinking toward them. She was wearing an eye-catching red strapless gown that showed off her sleek shoulders and flawless café-au-lait complexion. She was a woman who knew her captivating allure, but who also couldn't be trusted. Shane glanced back at Kayla and saw her rushing off toward the women's room.

"I'll go after her." Courtney had suddenly appeared from nowhere and went rushing after her older sister.

Shane stepped in, blocking Noelle's path from his family. "Noelle."

"Shane." Noelle smiled, revealing perfectly even white teeth. She leaned over and saw Kayla's retreating figure. "Your sister seems a little pale…. Or does that come from being nearly ready to give birth?"

"No thanks to you," Ethan hissed from Shane's side. Ethan looked as if he was ready to throttle her.

Noelle's almond-shaped eyes narrowed at Ethan. "Ethan. I'm so glad to see Kayla recovered after that fall. You know I had no idea she was pregnant."

"Would that have mattered to you, Noelle?" Shane responded before Ethan could answer. "She was married, but yet that didn't prevent you from coming to her home unannounced, trying to make a play for Ethan."

"Shane." Ethan touched his arm. "I got this."

"No, you don't," Shane replied and inclined his head to the women's room. "You go take care of your wife."

Ethan glanced at Noelle. He was ready to tell her a thing or two, but he decided to take Shane's advice instead and walked toward the restrooms.

"So you've aligned yourself with Andrew," Shane said. "What else are you up to, Noelle?" He had a feeling she wasn't done with the Adamses yet.

"I guess you'll just have to wait and see like everybody else." Noelle gave him a wink and sauntered away.

Kayla, Courtney and Ethan returned several minutes

later. "Are you okay? Is the baby okay?" Ethan was asking, remaining by her side.

"I'm fine." Kayla waved him away. She didn't see what all the fuss was about.

"Perhaps we should leave," Courtney suggested. She didn't want to see her sister hurt, especially by the likes of Noelle Warner. She'd been mistrustful of the actress from the start. No woman goes to work for her ex without an agenda.

"Absolutely not." Kayla shook her head. "I refuse to let Andrew Jackson think he got the better of us. He clearly has something under his sleeve and I, for one, want to see what it is."

Byron Adams scooted next to Kayla and gave her a gentle squeeze. "It's up to you, baby girl. If you want to stick it out, we will."

"I do," Kayla stated.

"Then let's go get 'em." Shane held his hand out to Kayla. She smiled at him and took his hand and Ethan's in her other.

Together, the Adams family walked into the ballroom.

Gabrielle had finished packing long ago. She sat waiting for the car Courtney had arranged to take her to the airstrip and was surprised when a knock sounded on her door.

Without looking at who it was, Gabrielle opened the door. "The bags are in here," she said, walking back into the living room.

"Gabby."

Gabrielle was startled to hear her mother's voice, and a soft gasp escaped her lips. She spun around to see if she was imagining it, but she wasn't.

Her mother stood in the flesh at the doorway, her eyes brimming with tears. "Oh, thank God I caught you."

"I'm tired, okay?" Gabrielle sighed, putting her hands up in defense mode. "I can't go another round with you. I said what I had to say in Marietta."

Her mother nodded, slowly walking toward her. "You had every right to be upset after the way we've treated you."

"What?" Gabrielle's mind reeled with confusion. "I don't understand."

"You were right, Gabby." Her mother walked toward her, but Gabrielle stepped backward, leaving her mother standing there, awkwardly clasping her hands. "Everything you accused us of was on the money. We've been cold, distant and unfeeling toward you for years. It was just that after Seth… We didn't know how to go on. But there you were every day, needing me. And I just couldn't get out of my own way to help you. You were grieving, too."

"I was." Gabrielle nodded in agreement. "Do you have any idea how hard it was for me to lose Seth? To know he sacrificed his life for me?" Her voice rose slightly. "I've had to live with survivor's guilt my entire life. And with the knowledge that it seemed like you guys wished it had been me who had died instead of Seth."

Her mother shook her head fervently. "No, honey, that's not true."

"It's how you made me feel," Gabrielle responded. "And the way you kept his room exactly the same, never changing it. It was like living with the memory of a ghost."

Her mother touched her chest. "That was all my fault. Your father wanted to take down the room and give everything to charity, but I couldn't bear it. He was my only son…"

"And I was your only daughter. A daughter you've forsaken—"

"—When we should have been cherishing you and showing you how much we loved you, and how thankful we were that you had survived," her mother finished. "But instead we pushed you away. I'm so sorry for hurting you, Gabby. I'm so sorry for the years I've wasted not knowing my own child. It took a lot of courage for you to finally stand there and tell us the crappy job we've done as your parents, but you did. And it broke my heart to hear you say you considered yourself an orphan. And that you were washing your hands of us forever."

"Is that why you're here?"

"Yes," her mother indicated. "I'm here to ask for your forgiveness and to see if there's a chance we could try and be mother and daughter again."

"I don't know…" Gabrielle said warily. "It might be a little too late. I don't know if I can forgive you *and Daddy.*"

"I'm not here to plead your father's case," her mother replied, "only mine. I guess I knew about your father's drinking and I turned a blind eye. But I was horrified to not only hear he had a gambling habit, which he'd covered up from me, but to hear what he'd done to you, his own child. So I asked your father to move out of the house."

"You did what?" Gabrielle struggled to comprehend what she'd just heard.

"Your father and I have separated. And I'm here today because I don't want you to leave without knowing that I love you with all my heart. And I'm truly sorry for all the pain I have caused you. I want you to know that you still have one parent left, if you'll have me."

Gabrielle's knees buckled underneath her and she fell to the floor, unnerved by the sudden change of events. She blinked in shock. To finally hear everything she'd wanted to hear her entire life was monumental.

Her mother came and touched her shoulder and Gabrielle looked up at her. "I know I don't deserve your forgiveness, Gabby, but I'm asking for it anyway. I love you so much and I thank God every day that I have you."

"Oh, Mama." Gabrielle grabbed her mother's knees and hugged her tight. "I've missed you so much," she cried.

"I know, baby." Her mother squatted down to her level and enveloped Gabrielle into a bear hug. "I have missed you so much."

They held each other for a long time, Gabrielle didn't know how long. Eventually, Gabrielle made it to the couch and she and her mother talked about why she was leaving Atlanta. Her mother was afraid of losing her again and asked her to stay.

"It's not that easy, Mama," Gabrielle replied. "I wish it were."

"Because you were fired?" her mother asked. "But you didn't do anything wrong. It was your father. Didn't you explain that to the Adamses?"

Gabrielle was silent.

"So you took the fall for him?" her mother surmised. "Oh, baby, you didn't have to do that. You've worked too hard to get where you are to go down like this."

"I know." Gabrielle hung her head low. "But as much as I'm angry with him, I didn't want him to get into any more trouble. Shane could tell I was covering for someone, and he didn't appreciate it one bit. And now Shane hates me, so I have to go."

"But if you explained everything…" her mother began.

"I doubt it would make much difference," Gabrielle replied. "Shane doesn't believe me or trust me."

"I'm so sorry, baby." Her mother hugged her. "But just know, wherever you are, you will always have me."

Gabrielle looked up through eyes laced with tears and said, "Thank you, Mama."

Chapter 15

The party at Jax Cosmetics continued much as all the other industry events Shane had been to. But then, just when he thought the evening would end with no further disasters, one of the Jax Cosmetics models walked past him and he got a whiff of her perfume.

Shane grabbed the woman's arm and she turned. "Sir, may I help you?" she asked, clearly frightened by Shane's aggression.

"What perfume are you wearing?" Shane asked, peering into her face.

The model smiled naughtily. "I can't tell you that. It's a secret."

Shane softened his grip on her arm and turned on the charm. "Of course you can, darling," he whispered and focused his eyes on her. Women could never resist his eyes. "There's nothing better than sharing a secret with someone else, is there? Then we'll both be in the know."

The young woman looked up at him. "Well," she said and blinked her eyelids several times. "It's the new Jax Cosmetics fragrance."

Shane fumed inside. Like hell it was. It was Ecstasy. He'd know the fragrance anywhere. Andrew had changed a couple of notes, so it wasn't exact, but it was still Shane's creation. And Jax Cosmetics had stolen it. "Thank you." Shane stroked her cheek and stormed over to where his family was congregated by the buffet table.

"Have you forgotten about Gabby so quickly?" Courtney asked when Shane approached. She'd seen him stroke the model's cheek.

"Not now, Courtney!" He pushed past her to their inner circle.

"What's wrong, son?" Elizabeth saw the distressed look on her son's face.

Shane was about to speak when Andrew Jackson appeared onstage.

"As CEO of Jax Cosmetics, I want to thank you all for coming tonight," he said loudly through the microphone. "We are excited about our fall product line. We have some lovely models walking around displaying our latest eye shadows and lipsticks. These are exciting new products that our consumers will love. Many of you have seen the placards placed throughout showcasing Academy Award–winning actress Noelle Warner. Noelle, would you come up here, please?"

Shane watched Noelle saunter to the stage. The audience burst into a big round of applause. Noelle bowed as if she was overcome by the outpouring, but Shane found it disingenuous considering she had been onstage with the Adams family just last year.

"We at Jax Cosmetics are determined to stay at the forefront of the industry, so effective immediately, Noelle will be appearing in our current ad campaign as the new Jax Cosmetics woman." Another round of applause. Once it had died down, Andrew continued, "But that isn't all...." He paused for effect. "We are excited to share that we are expanding into fragrance."

Shane glanced at Kayla and then Ethan. Without speaking, they knew the worst had happened. Shane expected smoke to come out of Ethan's ears any minute and Kayla looked defeated, but all Shane could feel was anxiety and he breathed in shallow, quick gasps. They'd suspected Andrew was behind the theft thanks to the picture with Gabby, but now they knew for sure.

"We've partnered with this beautiful woman here—" Andrew turned to Noelle "—to create the electric new fragrance. Everyone, I give you Noelle."

Screens around the room popped up with images of Noelle Wagner and Jax Cosmetics' first perfume Noelle in a cylinder-shaped bottle.

"The models around the room are wearing Noelle right now and are holding spritzers for everyone to smell. And as a special token of our appreciation, every guest this evening will receive a small sample. Enjoy, everyone!"

Shane felt sick as reporters swarmed the stage. "Mr. Jackson, you don't feel that Jax Cosmetics is imitating Atlanta's other local cosmetics giant, Adams Cosmetics, by coming out with a fragrance on the heels of their success with Hypnotic?"

Andrew turned and momentarily glared at the Adams family, before smiling back at the reporter. "Adams Cosmetics doesn't own the market on fragrance. There's room for all of us at the top, and with Noelle as the Jax woman—" he smiled at the actress, who'd left the stage to circulate "—I know we'll be a success."

"What the hell is going on?" Byron rushed over to

Shane's side. "What did Andrew do? I know he did something, so you might as well tell me."

Shane stared blankly at the stage where Andrew stood as his family started firing questions at him all at once.

Jax Cosmetics had a far-inferior chemist team than they had at AC. There was no way Andrew could have put together a fragrance, created the bottle and ad campaign and hired Noelle in such a short span of time. This had to have been planned for some time. He'd planned on stealing Shane's work.

"You don't need me to say it, Dad," Shane said.

"Shane?" His mother looked at him, but he couldn't meet her eyes. "Is it Ecstasy?" She knew Andrew hated their family, but just how far had he gone to hurt them?"

Shane nodded. "Yes, that's my fragrance up there." Shane pointed to the bottles on the screens. "He stole my work!"

"Ohmigod!" His mother's hand went to her mouth.

"That bastard," Byron yelled. "I'm gonna kill him." He charged toward the stage.

"Me first," Shane said, following his father. He would like nothing better than to rearrange Andrew Jackson's face for stealing his work. Andrew might be several inches taller, but Shane didn't care.

"Shane!" Kayla called out to her brother, but he and their father were already climbing the stage. "Ethan, do something!" She pushed her husband forward and soon he, too, was following behind them.

Andrew and Monica were standing on the stage looking smug when the men approached.

"I want to talk to you now, Jackson!" Bryon yelled.

"Not here," Monica said, eyeing the reporters in the room. "Why don't we take this elsewhere." She and Andrew left the stage and reluctantly Byron, Shane and

Ethan followed. Monica took them to a small room off the stage, where Jax Cosmetics was housing all its samples for the evening.

"You don't have any talent in your own family," Byron yelled, looking around the room, "so you have to steal from mine."

Andrew laughed. "Byron, is there a problem? You might want to be careful there. You know we can have heart attacks at our age."

"You know damn right there is a problem." Byron took a dangerous step forward and Andrew stepped back. "You stole our fragrance."

"Can you prove it?" Monica asked, folding her arms across her chest and standing by her stepfather. "Because I'm sure our attorneys will have a field day with this one."

"Proof won't matter," Ethan said, stepping forward. He walked up to Andrew until their faces were inches apart. "All we have to do is 'leak' it to the press and the appearance of impropriety will plunge your stock."

"Everyone in this industry knows that Jax Cosmetics is nothing but a two-bit copycat of Adams Cosmetics. You don't have half the talent I have in my baby finger." Shane held up his finger. "You may think you have gotten away with stealing my work, but mark my words, I will not rest until *I* destroy you."

"You both are using some mighty big words for a company that's about to go under," Andrew replied. "Perhaps you should be careful who you burn the next time around. Monica, let's go." He rushed his stepdaughter out of the room.

"What the hell did he mean by that?" Shane asked. He'd never burned anyone, but then he noticed Andrew headed straight to Noelle, and that's when it hit him. *He* hadn't burned anyone, but Ethan had.

"I could really kill that guy," Byron Adams said, "but I promised your mother. I'm going to go find her before I do something rash."

"I think that would be wise," Ethan replied. "What do you say we get out of here? I've had enough of Andrew Jackson for one evening." They all headed toward the door, but once they reached the ballroom, Shane pulled Ethan aside.

"Ethan, can I speak with you for a few minutes?"

Ethan turned around. "Sure, what's up?" He noted the serious look on Shane's face.

"I think we have our saboteur." Shane inclined his head toward Noelle.

"Noelle? What about her?" Ethan appeared to be confused.

"I haven't burned anyone recently," Shane said, "but you…"

"You think Noelle is somehow behind this?" Ethan asked. "Or is this your way of trying to absolve Gabrielle?"

"Honestly, I don't know what to believe," Shane responded. "I could have judged Gabrielle too quickly, and I never did give her the chance to explain. And we both know Noelle had reason to be upset. But how could she have gotten access?"

"There's only one way to find out," Ethan said and headed toward the stairs.

They returned to Kayla, Courtney and their mother, who were standing at the edge of the steps.

"I'm glad to see you didn't come to blows with Andrew," Elizabeth said. She was appalled by Andrew's behavior. He certainly held no resemblance to the man she'd once cared about.

"Trust me, I wanted to," Byron said, kissing her cheek. "But I promised you, and I don't lie to my wife."

Elizabeth smiled and brushed her lips across her husband's cheek.

Kayla looked back and forth at Ethan and Shane. Although they weren't speaking, their eyes said volumes. "What's up? What are you two *not* saying?"

"I think I know who's behind the theft," Shane whispered, "and we're going to go check out a hunch."

"Then you think it's not Gabby?" Courtney asked, eavesdropping on their conversation.

"Courtney." Shane sighed.

"Don't 'Courtney' me," she responded. "I have told you from day one that I thought you were wrong about Gabby. And I think you realize it, too."

"Now isn't a good time," Shane replied and headed toward the ballroom exit.

"There's never going to be a good time, Shane," Courtney returned, "especially when Gabby is gone."

Shane stopped in his tracks and spun around on his heels. "What are you talking about?"

"Gabby is leaving tonight. The company jet is scheduled to take off at 10:00 p.m. for an overnight flight."

"Leaving?" Shane asked, walking back to Courtney.

Courtney nodded. "Yes, she's had enough of you and her family and she's headed back to Paris, *indefinitely.*" She added the last word for effect. She didn't know for sure that Gabrielle was leaving for good and not coming back, but Shane didn't need to know that. Maybe it would light a fire under him if he knew he stood to lose her.

"I have to go." Shane abruptly fled the room.

"What was that all about?" their mother asked, coming toward her.

"I hope Shane is on his way to get his woman," Courtney replied as she watched her brother's retreating figure.

Shane and Ethan hailed a taxi and made it to Adams Cosmetics corporate offices in record time. They'd had to leave the limousine for the family's ride back to the mansion. Shane didn't care what time it was—he had to find out the truth. He had to find out if Noelle had stolen the fragrance and if he had falsely accused the woman he was in love with.

On his way to AC, he'd called ahead to the pilot and advised him to stall. He prayed that would buy him enough time to find out who was behind this mess. And if his gut instinct was right on this, he would have to plead for his life and beg Gabby not to leave him.

"Mr. Adams, Mr. Graham." The security guard sat up straight when they entered the building. "What are you doing here so late?"

"We need to ask you some questions," Shane said, "and see some security footage."

"Yes, sir, whatever you need," the guard replied.

"Has Noelle Warner been in this building in the past few months?" Shane asked.

"Sir?" The guard clearly was taken aback, and his eyes began shifting around the room instead of focusing on Shane.

"He asked when was the last time Ms. Warner was in the building," Ethan repeated. "And you'll want to answer this question honestly. Otherwise, there will be severe consequences."

"Well…" The guard looked down. "Ms. Warner came by the building a couple of months back claiming she'd forgotten some items she'd left behind when she was working here."

"Oh, she did, did she?" Shane looked at Ethan. They were finally getting to the truth.

"And?"

"And I let her upstairs in the executive offices."

"And what happened?"

"And then nothing," the guard replied. "I had to come back to my desk because the janitorial crew needed access to a locked office, and I keep the keys here. A little while later she returned with a box and then she was gone."

"Ohmigod!" Shane couldn't believe the guard's lackadaisical response, and he ran his fingers through his short fro. He'd accused Gabrielle falsely. She hadn't stolen the fragrance after all. Noelle had. "And you never thought to tell us this during our investigation of the leak of the prototype design or the formula theft?" Shane asked. "The incompetence here is unbelievable."

"Calm down, Shane." Ethan placed his hand on his brother-in-law's shoulder. "Let him finish."

"Don't calm me," Shane replied. "We accused Gabrielle of stealing when Noelle's the culprit!"

"We need to know more than just the guard's word," Ethan replied. "We need the camera footage. Do you remember the date Ms. Warner came in? And you had better not lie, because this is serious and could be criminal."

"I think so."

Ethan didn't waste any time contacting the head of security and, with his help, they figured out how to access the footage in question. The video showed Noelle in the AC lobby cozying up to the guard and then spilling his coffee over the counter. When he wasn't looking, another man took his security badge to access the lab. Minutes later, the DVD showed Noelle and the man in Shane's office. After zeroing in with the camera, it was revealed that the man, most likely a safecracker, manipulated the lock to obtain the combination to open the safe. Noelle then snapped a photo of the formula and planted it in Gabrielle's desk.

"This entire scheme was elaborate and deliberate," Shane replied.

"Noelle couldn't have thought of this on her own," Ethan replied. "She had to have had help."

"You know as well as I do that tying this to Andrew will not be easy," Shane said. "He's too slick and has covered his tracks."

"Even the slimy ones get caught," Ethan returned. "But if we have Noelle dead to rights on this, perhaps she'll give him up?"

"For you?" Shane's brow rose. "I doubt it."

"Her acts were criminal," Ethan replied harshly. "We can and will press charges. She'll have no choice."

"I'll let you handle that," Shane replied. "Right now, I have someplace to be." He glanced down at his watch and started retreating toward the door. The pilot had agreed to stall for a couple of hours, but said he'd have to take off since there were no more departures allowed after midnight.

Shane glanced down at his watch. He had only half an hour to get to the private airstrip. The guard had already called a taxi for him.

"You're going to get Gabrielle, aren't you?" Ethan asked, falling in beside Shane.

"How did you know?" Shane asked.

"I can tell a man in love. Because I had the same look when I thought I'd lost Kayla."

"I made a huge mistake accusing Gabrielle of stealing from us," Shane said once they'd made it outside. Thankfully, the taxi was waiting at the curb. "I should have known better," Shane said, opening the taxi door. "She doesn't have it in her to be deceptive."

"Sometimes it's easier to believe the bad in people versus the good," Ethan replied. "But you'll fix it. Go get her, tiger!"

Shane glanced sideways at Ethan and his pointed statement. It was the first time that they'd bonded over something other than work. "Thanks, man. I just pray it's not too late."

Gabrielle sighed as she looked around the lush private jet that belonged to Adams Cosmetics. She doubted the family would be happy about it, but it was a very generous offer from Courtney. She hadn't been looking forward to the long commercial flight in coach.

The evening had not gone as she'd planned. Her mother had shown up out of the blue to apologize and start anew. But Pamela Burton was finally showing some backbone and Gabrielle was impressed.

It wasn't going to be easy trying to forge a relationship after fifteen years, but Gabrielle had agreed to try. She told her mother she wasn't sure when she was coming back, but even if she didn't, she would fly her out to Paris so they could spend some time together.

And now she was sitting on the tarmac waiting. The pilot had informed her there was some kind of delay due to mechanical issues and so they'd sat for the past hour. Gabrielle was fine with it, as it gave her a chance to finally turn on her phone. There were several calls from Courtney and one from Shane that she promptly ignored.

Shane. The man she'd come to love, but who believed she was capable of sleeping with him one minute and deceiving him the next. Why would he call? Though she wasn't innocent by any means, since she hadn't told him the truth about her father leaking the bottle design, it still hurt knowing that he thought her capable of such manipulation. She'd given herself to him in every way imaginable. She'd held nothing back. Perhaps she should have protected herself better, but she hadn't.

She'd allowed herself to fall in love with Shane, with his brilliance, his caring nature, his gentleness, and it had all been snatched away from her in a heartbeat. Gabrielle didn't know what she was going to do, but she did know she needed some time and distance to figure it out. Meeting Mariah in Paris for some R&R sounded exactly like what she'd need after such a tumultuous few months back in the States.

Had she made a mistake in coming back? She'd tried to correct the mistakes of the past by reaching out to her parents, and it had nearly destroyed her. And Shane... Had it been a mistake to get involved with her boss and the one man she'd always secretly desired?

Suddenly, the jet door sprang open and Shane came running up the steps. He glanced around, and when his eyes landed on Gabrielle's, they lit up like a Christmas tree.

Gabrielle was momentarily shell-shocked and leaned back in the reclining seat. Was she imagining Shane because she so desperately wanted him to come for her and make a grand gesture?

"Shane? What are you doing here?" Gabrielle finally found her voice.

"I came here because I made a mistake."

"About?" His presence filled her with hope and apprehension.

"About you." Shane rushed toward her and kneeled down so he could face her.

"I don't understand." Confused, Gabrielle's eyes darted restlessly around the jet.

"I know you didn't steal the fragrance," Shane responded.

"You do?"

"It was Noelle Warner."

"The actress?" When Shane nodded, she asked, "Why?"

"It had nothing to do with me. She was once the face of Adams Cosmetics and we fired her because she tried to break up Ethan and Kayla's marriage. Needless to say, there's bad blood between her and Ethan."

"But how could she have gotten into the lab?"

"She used her feminine wiles on the guard, claiming she left something behind, and when his head was turned, she snatched his access card. Then she and a man accessed the lab and he cracked my safe."

"Ohmigod!" Gabrielle released a sigh of relief. "So, are you going to press charges?"

"Absolutely, Ethan was adamant about it, but I wasn't about to stay and find out," Shane replied. "I just knew I had to catch you before you left."

"You should have just let me go," Gabrielle said, pushing up from the chair and rising to her feet. Shane did the same.

"Why would you say that?"

"Because nothing has changed," Gabrielle replied. "So, I'm not guilty of stealing the fragrance, but what about the photo of the prototype?"

Shane paused. Gabby was right. There was the issue of the prototype design, and there was no evidence that Noelle had leaked it to the press.

"Ask me, Shane," Gabrielle taunted. "Ask me again."

"Okay, Gabby, why don't you tell me what happened with the photo of the prototype?"

"Are you finally ready to listen?" Gabrielle inquired.

"Yes, I am."

"Good, because I didn't do it."

"I know that," Shane replied. "But you know who did. And knowing all of that, I am still here asking you not to leave. I believe we have something special, Gabby, but I need you to trust me. I need you to tell me who did it, Gabby."

"And how can I believe we have something worth salvaging when you can so easily believe that I deceived you and stole from your family? Why don't you tell me that, huh?"

Shane paused for several long seconds. "That's a fair question. And I guess we're both going to have to take a leap of faith and trust in each other. I'm not perfect, Gabby. I'm going to make mistakes, and I admit this one is a doozy. In my heart of hearts I knew you weren't capable of lying to me."

"Then why did you believe it?"

Shane shook his head. "I don't know if I ever really did. I was just in so much pain. I think it was easier for me to believe the worst in you, because if I did, then I wouldn't have to confront the feelings I was having for you."

"Which are?"

"That I've fallen in love with you, Gabby Burton."

Gabrielle looked at him with surprise and utter astonishment. She hadn't in her wildest dreams expected Shane to admit he loved her as she loved him. It filled her with so much joy that she felt she might burst. But it scared her, too. She knew all too well what it was like to have love and lose it. Her relationship with her parents had taught her that. "Love?"

Shane smiled. "Yes, love… I think I knew when we

were at the chateau. My family sure as hell saw it, but I think I was afraid to believe it, to let it in."

"And now you do, because you have proof I didn't steal from you? How can I be sure that you won't change your mind?"

Shane walked toward Gabrielle and held both sides of her face. "I guess you're going to have to believe me, baby, when I tell you that I love you. Because it's true. And I know you may not believe me now, because I hurt you. And I'm sorry about that. I truly am. All I can ask is for your forgiveness."

"I do forgive you, Shane." Gabrielle fought back the tears. "And I love you, too."

"You love me?" Shane was overcome with emotion. His lips claimed hers, moving over them and devouring their softness. He crushed Gabby to him, eager to remember the sleek curves of her luscious body against his hard one. He'd known Gabby cared for him when she'd said as much at his loft, but he hadn't dared hope that she felt the same as he did, especially after the boorish way he'd behaved toward her.

When Shane finally lifted his head, Gabrielle nodded through eyes glazed with tears, "I've been crazy about you for a long time, Shane, and once I came back to the States and really got to know you, I fell for you hard and fast. So much so that I didn't want to lose you by telling you the truth about my family."

"What truth?"

"That my father deceived me," Gabrielle replied. She felt as if she could finally be honest about her family, about her history, about all of it. "He came to my apartment acting like he wanted to make amends for the past, but he was just using me. *He* stole the photo of the prototype, Shane, not me."

"Your father stole the image of the prototype?"

Gabrielle nodded. "My father works for Jax Cosmetics. He has for years, and when he developed a drinking and gambling problem, Andrew used it to his advantage. He even tried to blackmail me into spying on AC for him."

Understanding dawned on Shane. "That's why you were photographed with him?"

"And when I refused to do his bidding, he vowed to use our meeting as evidence against me."

"And I fell for it!" Shane couldn't believe how gullible he'd been. But then again, Andrew Jackson was a master manipulator.

"It wasn't your fault," Gabrielle responded. "I have to take the blame, too. I should have been honest with you from the start about my family's connection to Andrew Jackson, but I wasn't. I contributed to your lack of faith in me. I was just so desperate to believe my father and I could have a relationship that I refused to see what was right in front of my face. But now I understand that he doesn't deserve my love and trust. Trust is something that's earned. But my Mom… There might be hope for us yet. She came to me tonight asking if we could start over, and I agreed to try."

"That's wonderful news about your mom." Shane pulled her into his arms and held her close. "But I'm so sorry that your father betrayed you, baby. But, it's all out in the open now. There're no more secrets between us."

"None."

"Then we can start fresh?"

"I would like that very much." Gabrielle eyes were brimming with tears.

"Good, because not only has Courtney and the rest of the Adams family missed you—" Shane bent down to kiss the tip of her nose, then her eyes and then her satisfyingly soft mouth "—but I've missed you, too, in the lab and in my bed."

"Oh, really," Gabrielle replied and found Shane's eyes smoldering with fire as he pulled her into his arms.

"Yes, and I can't wait to show you just how much." Shane grinned naughtily before covering her mouth hungrily with his.

"And I look forward to it," Gabrielle responded as Shane wrapped her in a silk cocoon of pure euphoria.

Epilogue

"I can't believe how successful Ecstasy's launch was to-night," Gabrielle commented as she and Shane lay on his leather sofa at his loft after a long evening full of family, networking and press. They'd stayed longer than expected at the launch party because new-mom Kayla couldn't bear to be separated from her two-month-old son, Alexander, so she and Ethan had sneaked off to spend more time with him. They'd left Courtney at the party eating up the spot-light. Of course Gabrielle and Shane owed her big-time, because she'd been instrumental in bringing the two of them together.

"I can," Shane replied, rubbing Gabby's feet, which she'd complained were hurting her after an evening spent in four-inch heels. "Thanks to you—" he pinched her nose "—we delivered a high-quality product."

Gabrielle smiled. "I only gave you a couple of notes. You did all the heavy lifting."

"But I couldn't have done it without you," Shane said, planting a tender kiss on her slightly parted lips.

The caress of Shane's lips on hers set Gabrielle's body aflame as it always did, and her heartbeat began to sky-rocket.

"We're a team, you and me," Shane said, lifting her suddenly into the cradle of his arms. In a short time, Gabrielle had come to mean more to him than any woman ever had. He couldn't imagine his life without her. When she wasn't with him, he missed her. He missed her smile, her passion for the lab and her warmth when she was lying next to him. He'd thought he could never find a woman who lived up to his mother, but Gabby had. She was beautiful, smart and loyal, and he wanted her as a permanent fixture in his life. He lifted himself slightly off the couch, so he could reach inside his pants pocket for a small black box.

"Yes, we are." Gabrielle's mouth curved into a smile.

"Which is why—" Shane held out the box "—I want to marry you."

"Excuse me?" Gabrielle was floored and turned in his arms, so she could see his face. Was he serious? They'd been inseparable for months, but she hadn't expected a proposal.

Shane lifted Gabrielle and shifted off the couch, so he could bend down on one knee for a proper proposal. "Gabrielle Marie Burton, I love you more than I could have ever imagined, and I want to spend the rest of my life with you. Will you marry me?" He opened the black box to reveal a cushion-cut solitaire ring with diamond band from Tiffany's. It was stylish, yet classic and simple, like Gabby.

"Yes!" Gabrielle jumped in Shane's arms. "Yes, I will marry you."

"Then allow me." Shane pulled back slightly, so he

could slide the ring on her finger. "I love you, Gabby, and I promise to love you always." He bent down and sealed his vow with a slow, drugging kiss that sent shivers of desire running up Gabrielle's spine.

"I love you, too, Shane Adams."

* * * * *

REQUEST YOUR FREE BOOKS!

2 FREE NOVELS
PLUS 2 **FREE GIFTS!**

KIMANI™
ROMANCE

Love's ultimate destination!

 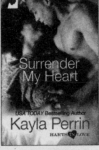